PRAISE FOR *SONGS FOR A TEENAGE NOMAD*

"*Wow!* Rich, beautifully detailed, extremely well written, and completely real people in a real world coping, just as we all cope. Calle is a female kind of Holden Caulfield…Brilliant work."
—*Ben Franklin Award judge*

"This is a novel that you will want to experience over and over again, just like a great song."
—*Teensreadtoo.com 5-Star Review by Becca Boland*

"Culbertson has crafted a world true and honest to the teenage experience, with characters you love immediately."
—*Loretta Ramos, MFA Producers Program,*
UCLA School of Theater, Film, and Television

"I can't imagine anyone not liking this book. Using music in a teen book contributes to the authenticity of the story. I think there are many, many teens that will see themselves in this book, and it will help to validate who they are."
—*Ben Franklin Award judge*

"As if being a freshman in high school isn't hard enough, Calle Smith has to endure a rootless life with a mother who can't seem to settle down in one town or with one guy. Told through a blend of prose, song lyrics, and musical references, *Songs* tells the story of a girl whose life resembles a random-shuffle playlist struggling to become comfortable in her own skin."

—azTeen Magazine *Book Club selection*

"Culbertson writes with great respect for teenagers. Her literary yet accessible prose is both thoughtful and entertaining, an engaging blend of humor and heartbreak. The book speaks not just to teenagers but also to their parents—to anyone who has been young and searching for their own soundtrack."

—*Rebecca Kochenderfer, senior editor, Homeschool.com, coauthor of* Homeschooling for Success

"In *Songs for a Teenage Nomad*, Kim Culbertson expertly captures the tumultuous adolescent experience."

—Maui Time Weekly

"Culbertson gives an independent voice to the teen genre."

—*Tyler Midkiff,* Sedona Red Rock News

WHAT READERS ARE SAYING

"Kim Culbertson understands me. I hear my own voice—my own confusion, pain, happiness, and self-discovery—echoed through Calle's narrative. From start to finish, I related to Calle on a level that I have never before experienced in a book."

—*Michaela, Portland, Oregon*

"I absolutely loved it! I laughed; I cried…it was just such a great book. It was so relatable."

—*Ashley, Sausalito, California*

"Kim Culbertson's book was absolutely fantastic! It's beautifully written with thought-provoking passages that make you laugh, wonder, and cry. I loved this book because I understand what Calle is going through—I have been there, and at times I feel that this book is describing me. Filled with music and memories, you are sucked in. I couldn't stop reading! Calle learns to deal with her turbulent life, the people around her, and a past she has never had a chance to face. This book is one to be read again and again. Eloquent and filled with truth, this is a story that will stay with you forever."

—*Laura, Hawaii*

"This book was astounding! It was incredibly relatable to me as a reader, and it is wonderfully written. I love Kim Culbertson's book, and I am positive that it is a story that will stay with me forever!"

—*Sydney, age 16, Grass Valley, California*

AWARDS

Ben Franklin Awards 2008, Winner, Best New Voice in Children's and Young Adult Fiction category

2008 Next Generation Indie Book Awards, Winner, Young Adult Fiction category

2008 Independent Publisher Book Awards, Silver Medal Award Winner, Juvenile–Young Adult Fiction category

London Book Festival 2007, Winner, Teenage category

National Best Books 2007 Awards, Award-Winning Finalist in the Fiction & Literature, Young Adult Fiction category

2007 DIY Book Festival Awards, Honorable Mention, Teenage category

SONGS
FOR A
TEENAGE
NOMAD

KiM CULBERTSON

sourcebooks
fire

Published by Sourcebooks Fire, an imprint of Sourcebooks, Inc.
P.O. Box 4410, Naperville, Illinois 60567-4410
(630) 961-3900
Fax: (630) 961-2168
teenfire.sourcebooks.com

Library of Congress Cataloging-in-Publication Data

Culbertson, Kim A.
  Songs for a teenage nomad / by Kim Culbertson.—1st ed.
     p. cm.
  Summary: Having lived in twelve places in eight years, fourteen-year-old Calle Smith knows
better than to put down roots, storing memories in a song journal while she keeps the world at
a distance, but friends—even a boyfriend—are there to help when she learns why her mother
has always been on the run.
  [1. Moving, Household—Fiction. 2. Mothers and daughters—Fiction. 3. Memory—Fiction.
4. High schools—Fiction. 5. Schools—Fiction. 6. Fathers and daughters—Fiction. 7. Family
life—California—Fiction. 8. California—Fiction.] I. Title.
  PZ7.C8945Son 2010
  [Fic]—dc22
                                                   2010014381

Printed and bound in the United States of America.
VP 10 9 8 7 6 5 4 3 2 1

FOR PETER

PROLOGUE

"...HEY, MR. TAMBOURINE MAN, PLAY A SONG FOR ME. IN THE JINGLE JANGLE MORNING, I'LL COME FOLLOWIN' YOU..."
—BOB DYLAN

Inside my dreams sits a song, way back in the shadows. It calls to me, and I wait to know it in the daylight, wanting to pull it like taffy from the haunts of my mind. Somehow, my memories begin with this song. I can't seem to put an image to it; it's a memory blurred and swirling, with no shape...

CHAPTER 1

GET OUT THE MAP

...the air smelling like honeysuckle, I dangle my arm from the passenger window, aware only of the honeysuckle air, Indigo Girls on a scratchy radio, and a white sun. And that everything we own has been packed into the back of a battered orange moving van...again...

"MY DAD NAMED ME CALLE after a cat he had in college that ran away. He really loved that cat. I always thought that was funny since he was the one who ran away from me...and my mom."

"Calle? With just the "e" at the end? Not C-A-L-L-I-E?" the counselor asks.

"Just an 'e.' It's how he spelled the cat's name. The Smith part's easy, though."

Mr. Hyatt, the counselor, shifts in his seat and scribbles something on a yellow legal pad. He has on a Mickey Mouse tie and red shoes. Vans. I've seen the uniform before. Mickey tie because he has to wear a tie but doesn't want students to think he's stuffy. Vans because they're Vans. The nameplate on his desk says "Hyatt Way," like a street sign.

I watch him write, making sure I don't say more than I should. I always give away too much information, and sometimes it gets me in trouble. My mother once said I inherited this from my father. I don't remember him, have never even seen his picture. I take her word for it. And don't ask questions about him. It just makes her mad.

But the talking thing. I'm working on it. I've always admired the type of kid who can sit in silences and not need to fill them. There is one of those silences now.

"Your mom is remarried?" He flips through the manila folder with my name written in black marker on the tab.

"Yeah. Rob."

"Rob," he repeats, over-rounding the letters. Raawwbb. Annoying.

"He works in computers and stuff." Actually, I have no idea what Rob does for a living, but I figure he probably has a computer wherever he works. He married my mom a month ago in San Diego where we used to live. She'd known him only four months. Now we live here. Andreas Bay, a snag in the Northern California coastline. The only thing I know is that he drives a Ford like all the others and makes a bunch of promises like all the others.

"How'd you guys end up in Andreas Bay?" Mr. Hyatt looks up from my folder, his pen poised.

"Same way we find every town. My mom tosses a penny onto a map of California, and we go wherever it lands." He nods and pretends this isn't strange. Usually that story gets at least a raised eyebrow.

He finishes writing, caps his pen, and pushes my new schedule across the desk. "You like to write?" He points at the journal in my lap, with its faded purple velvet cover that looks like corduroy pants.

I instinctively clasp a hand over the cover. "It's my song journal."

"Song journal?"

"Last year, I started writing down memories I get from songs. I hear one, mostly older songs, and I write down the memory it brings. Like glimpses of my life as I remember it. Snapshots." His nod is directed over my shoulder. A black-haired girl in a Betty Boop T-shirt and skinny jeans hovers by the door. I shrug. "It's just something I do."

"Cool. Sounds really cool." Trying too hard.

"My mom's not the type to keep photo books. So I sort of have to keep my own version."

I don't tell him I'm hunting for the Tambourine Man who plagues my dreams.

• • •

"You're sure you don't want a nicer shirt to wear?"

In the mirror, I look at my mother, perched on the side of the tub, holding a coffee mug the size of her head. Her dark hair is wet from the shower and combed back away from her face.

I spit toothpaste into the sink. "I like what I'm wearing," I say for the third time. Swirling water around my mouth, I stare at my reflection. Faded blue T-shirt, jeans, brown eyes, shoulder-length brown hair. I look the same as I always do. A blurry, ordinary version of the beauty sitting behind me.

People say I look like her but it's in an out-of-the-corner-of-your-eye sort of way. We both have dark hair and eyes, but her genes lined up in the right order; her dark hair thick, her eyes wide. Her angles drawn straight, her limbs long. My genes used some sort of splatter method for me, with everything not quite in the right spot. People notice my mom no matter what she's doing. If I wanted to be noticed, which I usually don't, I'd have to hire a band and some fireworks.

"First days are so critical," she continues, sipping out of her trough.

I catch her eye in the mirror. "I think I know something about first days."

This shuts her up. For about one second.

"You'll be fine," she says. "It's like riding a bike."

"What is?"

"First days."

I roll my eyes. My mother has a tendency to launch into speeches that start sounding like the bad television she watches. I say nothing. I don't want to encourage her.

"The school is beautiful," she says, trying a different tack.

I nod, leaning in to inspect what looks like it might be a pimple on my left cheekbone. "Ocean view. Not bad."

"You'll really like it here." She tightens the sash of her yellow terry robe with her free hand. "It's a really nice town. Small, independently owned stores. A real community."

"You've been reading way too many billboards for subdivisions off the freeway," I say.

She frowns into her coffee. "I just think it's really cute. Rob loves it here."

"Rob sits in an office all day. He eats boring for breakfast."

"Calle…" I can see her start to falter, the tears just around the corners of her large eyes.

I back off.

"It's great," I say, and she smiles over her coffee. "Cute." Though I wonder how cute it will be when she realizes that she's not a tourist and that she actually lives here.

I take a last look in the mirror before walking into the hallway for my backpack. She follows me out, her bare feet slapping against the ceramic tiles. "You're sure you don't want to borrow my red shirt with the Buddha? The cute one with three-quarter-length sleeves?"

"I'm sure," I say, slinging my backpack over my shoulder and trying not to roll my eyes. Two years ago in seventh grade, she convinced me to wear a green dress the first day. I spent the next four months as "Gumby." No thanks.

She gives up. "Okay, sweetie." She leans over to give me a peck on the cheek, the one that's not getting a pimple. "Good luck on your first day!"

I open the door and smile back at her. She looks genuinely hopeful for me, the way she always does when we come to a new place. She even packed me a lunch.

"Thanks," I say, holding up the brown sack. Giving a little wave, I pull the front door closed behind me.

Outside, drowning out the sound of gulls, I pull on my headphones—Jack Johnson's guitar soothing the frenzy of nerves in my gut—and begin the eight-block walk to school, buoyed by the cool sea air. I take in the green hills and the small, flat-roofed houses, and spot a flash of ocean as I round the last corner toward the school. It's actually one of the more beautiful places we've landed, and I sigh, wondering how long I'll get to have this view.

CHAPTER 2

SMALL TOWN

...my mother turns the radio up because she has always been in love with John Cougar Mellencamp, insists on the Cougar part of his name, even if the singer has dropped it. We sprawl on the sloping lawn of the park, my mother letting her lunch break run way long. Light glints off her silver-rimmed sunglasses as she hands me half a tuna sandwich with extra pickles...

MY NEW SCHOOL SMELLS LIKE pickles, salty, and clogged with a sea of faces that all look the same. The campus stands on a low hill facing the ocean. Across the road from the main office where I babbled to Mickey Mouse Tie, there's a small strip of buildings: a café, a hair salon, a movie rental place, and a doctor's office whose large brick walls keep the students away from the coast.

I watch the students clumped around me in their between-classes packs. I stay close to a row of outside lockers, wedging myself between the bathrooms and the library building. I want a good view of the quad without being too much out in the open. Even here, I can feel people eye me. The new girl. No matter how many times I've done this, my stomach is always full of bees. Newness is nothing like riding a bike. Your body has no memory of it, and it doesn't end with a fun ride.

My eyes fall on a group of girls in short skirts who are laughing with some boys. A zipper-thin girl with a thick blond ponytail has her arm draped casually around a dark-haired boy in a blue and green football jersey. Popular. I look away. I realized by third grade I would never be one of those girls. I'm not tiny or bouncy. I'm cursed with big bones and one-toned brown hair that refuses to fall the way it should. Not like their hair, lightened, glossy, and smelling of flowers and fruit. Even when I buy special shampoo, my hair smells like hair.

And fashion. Not a chance. I have a midriff that doesn't want to break dress-code rules and no money to finance a wardrobe worthy of notice. So I wear my standard uniform of jeans and a T-shirt, with a sweatshirt if it's cold out. I have an old gray sweatshirt with holes around the cuffs that I can wear and wear and never get sick of.

But I don't hate those girls with their color-coded outfits, with their rules and gossip and fashion-magazine group quizzes: "Is He Cheating?!" They invent complicated lives because their lives aren't that complicated. I prefer my holes-in-the-cuffs sweatshirt.

The bell rings for third period. Damn. I spaced out trying to disappear. I look around me. The sea of faces has rinsed into the surrounding classrooms like water down a drain, and I am left alone with a warm sun and no idea where I'm supposed to be. I look at my schedule and then walk all the way around the squat, box-like 400 building twice, looking for Room 406, Freshman English. But all the rooms are numbered in random order, with 405 next to 410 and then 407. No 406.

"You lost?"

A voice from behind startles me. I turn. The boy is skinny and smooth-skinned. He wears black jeans and a black shirt that says in bold white lettering, "pissing off the planet one person at a time." He points at my schedule. "Do you need help?"

"Room 406." My voice sounds high in the quiet air. This is the fastest anyone has ever spoken to me at a new school. At Hamilton Middle in Manteca, no one said a word to me the whole first week. A personal record. "Who numbers these stupid rooms?"

"Monkeys. Room 406?" He doesn't have a backpack or any books. "The Cell. Follow me. I have that class too. I'm Drew, by the way."

"Calle." I follow him down a hallway into the center of the building. "You're a freshman?" He seems way older and walks like he's been here awhile.

"Not really." He turns and smiles a mouth full of straight white teeth. Orthodontically straight. "I flunked Freshman English last year. Repeat offender."

"Oh."

He pushes open the door to 406. The windowless room is pasted floor to ceiling with movie posters. Jennifer Lopez's glossy face from *The Cell* provides a centerpiece.

"Mr. Billings." A youngish man in a tie at the front of the room looks up from a roll sheet. "Nice of you to join us."

"I was helping the new girl find your room." Drew glances around. "I like what you've done with the place."

The teacher tries not to smile. "Thanks," he says.

Aware of the eyes locked on me from the various round tables in the room, I shift my weight and look around. Blond Ponytail Girl from earlier sits at a nearby table, twirling a lock of her hair around and around her finger while smiling coyly at the dark-haired boy next to her. The boy catches my eye, smiles slightly, and then focuses on Blond Girl. My stomach flutters as his hazel eyes flit back to me.

"You're Cal, then?" The teacher mispronounces my name. I look away from the boy. Mr.—I check my schedule—Ericson. Not his fault, though—no "i."

"Call-*e*. Sorry I'm late. I couldn't find the room." My eyes wander around the classroom. My last English class had perfectly even rows, and a teacher who smelled like oranges and cigarettes.

"Just don't make it a habit." He pauses, checking something off on his clipboard, and then continues. "Well, welcome, Calle. You and your knight in shining armor can have a seat over here." Mr. Ericson gestures to a round table next to Blond Girl. A red-haired girl dressed in black sits alone at the table, softly sketching on her binder.

As we scoot by, my backpack grazes a girl in a purple tank top sitting next to Blond Girl.

"Hey!" she yelps, clutching the back of her head as if burned.

"Sorry," I say, quickly slipping into my seat, cheeks flaming.

"Don't worry," the redhead at my table says, not looking up from her binder. "Nothing in that head to damage."

"Bite me, Alexa," Purple Tank Top hisses.

Alexa smiles.

I sink down in my seat, glancing at the next table. Is it my imagination, or did the boy smile too?

• • •

"You gotta eat, right?" Drew finds me several periods later.

"Wow, Mr. Welcoming Committee." I try to sound casual, but inside I am flying. I've never had a lunch invite on the first day. Last year, at Bell Middle, I spent the first day's lunch period in the nurse's office with a fake stomachache.

"Follow me."

We weave our way through the clumps of students sitting on the lawn in front of the school toward a large gnarled tree. It casts an arc of shade, its roots spilling onto the sidewalk that separates the road from the lunching teenagers. I stare closely at the group of students lounging under the tree, recognizing the red-haired girl we sat with in English. Alexa. She laughs at something a boy in a Weezer shirt says and flips her head, as if her cropped hair had not always been so short.

"Hello, AN-drew," drawls a round-faced boy. He sits with his back to the tree, his hand jammed into a bag of Cheetos. "Who's your friend?" His jeans balloon around him down to frayed edges, exposing remarkably thin pink ankles and banana-yellow flip-flops.

A girl in a tight, black tank top squints up at us. "You picking up strays again, Drew?" she asks smiling. I can't read her, can't tell if she's joking. I might end up back in the nurse's office after all, only this time I won't be faking it.

But Drew ignores her. He's suddenly the MC of the tree crowd, announcing me, his wrist covered thickly with brightly colored rubber bracelets. "This is Calle. She's from San Diego. She listens to sucky music, but we won't hold it against her. I flush. Drew had pawed through my CD case during English, declaring each disc "Crap!" He now sees my face. "Hey, no judgment."

Everyone has their own version of hello. Even Black Tank Top gives a wave as she flips through a day planner.

"Have a seat." A girl in a lime-green T-shirt and jeans pats the ground next to her. "I'm Tala." Her hair is pulled into elaborate twists and braids like a *Star Wars* princess. Her whole face smiles.

"Hi." I settle on the ground next to her, removing my lunch from my bag, my stomach churning.

Black Tank Top snaps the planner shut and eyes me closely. "I'm Sara," she says, not unfriendly, but not with the same sweetness as Tala. Her eyes are the prettiest shade of green I have ever seen, deep and yellow flecked. She's older than the others, maybe even a senior. And she has cleavage. Real cleavage.

"Nice to meet you," I say, pulling apple slices from my lunch bag and trying not to stare at the cleavage, even though I think that's kind of the point.

She nods, taking small bites from her peanut butter sandwich, and shifts her gaze to the note she's unfolded in her lap.

Drew settles himself next to me and looks around. "Where's Toby?"

"Cigarette." Cheetos Bag informs on him.

"Gaven?"

"Kissing Hecca's ass." Sara makes a face. "Auditions aren't even until next week, and he's already picking a monologue."

Drama kids. They're at every school. Reading Shakespeare for fun, dressed in black, talking about famous directors. Ignoring the rest of us. I have no idea what to say to them.

Sara turns to me. "Do you act?" Her voice has a competitive edge.

Alexa, the girl from English, looks at her pointedly. "Not everyone under this tree has to act, Sara."

"I was just *asking*." She looks back at me, rolling her eyes. "Alexa gets pissy when we say 'act.'" She makes little quotation mark signs in the air with her fingers. "She's a stage manager and set designer."

"I've never acted," I tell them, unless my recurring role as New Girl counts. I tried out for a play once in sixth grade. Well. Not exactly. I stood on a blank stage and held the paper we were supposed to read from, my legs shaking. Then Missy Pinkle started giggling in the front row, whispering something to Erica Jenson, and I ran from the stage. No one liked Missy Pinkle—she was a stuck-up, prissy snob—but it didn't matter. I haven't been on stage since.

Sara stares at me like I have a disgusting bug on my face. "Are you in drama?"

"No."

She glances at Drew. "Oh. Well." She sucks in her lower lip, looking back at me. "That's cool." She eyes my journal, her first real smile of the day breaking through. "Oh! You're a writer." She smiles again and pops open an orange soda. "We do student-written plays in the spring."

I don't tell her that for me the spring is a long way off.

"Hey, guys," says a voice behind us.

The whole group turns. A boy with black-ink-marker hair flops down next to Drew. He has Asian lines to his eyes and freckles across his pale skin. It's actually a relief to see this kid. This town's so white it makes Wonder Bread look multi-grain.

"What did the Buddhist monk say to the hot dog vendor?" The black-haired boy asks, a smile already coming across his face.

"I don't know, Eli," Sara says. "What?"

"Make me one with everything." He beams, looking hopefully around the group. Cheetos Bag laughs, kicking his flip-flopped feet into the ground.

I laugh too, watching the boy closely. He notices, reaches across Drew, and offers his hand. "Eli."

I shake it. "Calle." He doesn't let go right away, just nods and repeats my name.

"Eli wants to be a stand-up comedian," Tala explains, her gaze curious as it slips between us.

"What'll your day job be?" I say, smiling at him. I instantly regret it and carefully remove my hand from his grasp. But his smile widens, his dark eyes soft, studying me, and something in his gaze makes me flush clear to my ears.

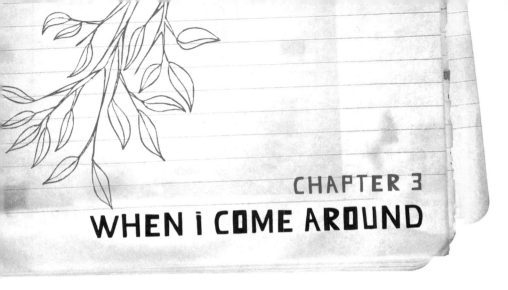

CHAPTER 3

WHEN i COME AROUND

...Mom screaming at me to turn Green Day down. Rob has a headache. We've known Rob three days, and he already gets to be the volume police. I sprawl on the lawn, the sky above me tangerine, lighted tropical colors everywhere, like the world has been swallowed by a mango smoothie...

THE BOX SITS IN MY lap, but I'm afraid to open it. The wood is smooth, the color of cream, heavily polished. There is no lock. I have never seen this box before.

And I wasn't supposed to find it. I'm certain of that.

When I got home from school today, I just wanted Golden Grahams in my favorite bowl. The ceramic one with the duck painted on the side that I made at one of those paint-it-yourself places with my mom's ex-boyfriend, Blue Aerostar Greg, when I was eight. He had outlined the duck for me in black, and I painted in the yellow. Greg was the only one of my mom's boyfriends who wrote a note with my name on it when he left.

They all drove away in Fords, but he was the only one who left a note just for me.

But I couldn't find the bowl. Instead, I found this box. Shoved against the back of the shelf over the stove. I sit on the counter with it in my lap, all around me the sound of the empty kitchen. I'm supposed to be getting ready for the Welcome Back Dance at school. I hate dances, but Drew and Alexa talked me into going.

I open the box.

Inside, I discover some of my mother's old driver's licenses, all with different married names and various hairstyles. Mom blond. Mom with braids. Always smiling, newly married, hopeful. Before everything goes wrong. There is a Polaroid of me at my tenth birthday with chocolate cake all over my face. I smile at the memory. The first and last time my mother baked my birthday cake from scratch. I ate it, even though it tasted like sand.

Under the picture, nestled in a curl of blue silk ribbon she used to tie in my hair, is a gold wedding band. A man's band. Maybe Red Mustang Ted's. I'm pretty sure she sold all the others. Sometimes when it doesn't work out, Mom's not as sad as other times. She was sad after Red Mustang Ted. It's probably his. I find a smooth rock from Arizona and a key with a plastic tag that reads "Waves Inn." We stayed in that run-down inn near the beach for two weeks after Mom split with Nick, a personal trainer she met in Santa Barbara who always wore workout suits and way too much musk cologne. Neither of us misses Nick. Even if he did drive a very sweet '67 Ford Fairlane.

There are a few more pictures that other people must have taken.

SONGS FOR A TEENAGE NOMAD

My mom is in all of them in various smiling poses. In them, she is the light in the room. She's always the light in the room. Until the current guy leaves. I've never been able to guess when he'll leave. I just know he will. I flip through the rest of the pictures. I'm not in any of them.

Shrugging, I push everything aside. Another box, small and dark, rests at the bottom. A music box. Small, gold flowers curl around the broken lock. I open it. The music box part has been removed, revealing black velvet that has been cut away in places.

Nestled there is a single black-and-white photograph. A man. Dark-eyed. Smiling at the camera beneath a white cloudless sky. He wears a pea coat with the collar turned up against a wind that tousles his hair. "Jake," it says on the back, and below that, "Winter."

My breath catches. I have his eyes, and I see myself in the hard line of his jaw. A picture of Jake Smith. My father. Under a white winter sky.

. . .

Music pulses hollowly as we walk through the doors. Small, white twinkle lights trail like ivy around the walls of the gym. A makeshift dance floor covers the gym to half court where a curtain has been pulled to separate the gym into two parts. The basketball hoops have been pulled up into dark, crouching vultures in the rafters.

Drew wrinkles his nose. "Smells like feet," he says above the din of Duran Duran. "*Welcome to the Awesome '80s*," says a sign hanging on the far wall.

Toby and Tala move past me. I just met Toby outside, and I'm convinced he's really too tall to look at. Tala's neck must hurt all the time. He sees the sign and frowns at Tala. "You didn't tell me about the '80s theme."

Smiling, Tala squeezes his hand. "You wouldn't have come," she says, pointing to Eli and Alexa standing by the snack table.

"They're supposed to be watching movies at Sara's," Drew mumbles. I'm quickly discovering that Drew hates to be out of the loop. We follow him across the semi-empty dance floor, Toby and Tala's hands laced together in a casual weave of fingers.

"What's up?" Drew asks Eli.

Eli pops the top from an Oreo and licks the white middle. He hands the cookie top to Alexa. "Sara only wanted to watch *Fight Club* for the ten-millionth time. I refuse to watch Brad Pitt's naked torso anymore. Besides, there's food here." He pauses. "Hey, Calle."

"Nice outfit."

Eli always seems to be in something leather or plastic, a vinyl shirt, slick pants, or the thick bracelets he wears on both wrists like manacles. Tonight, he wears black pleather head to toe and a pair of red Converse sneakers. Leather ones.

"Thanks." He leans forward to pluck another Oreo from the stack. A blush deepens the smatter of freckles on his face.

I smile, feeling off balance in this new place with the music around me and the warmth of all the bodies. I'm still reeling from the first glimpse of my father. His picture is tucked away in the folds of my song journal, but I put the box back over the stove. No need for Mom to know I found him. Not yet. Before the dance, I plugged Jake Smith into Google, but more than fifteen million results came up. Where to start? My father might be somewhere in those pages of people and lives.

"We need to talk." Alexa cuts into my thoughts, pulling my arm and starting toward the bathroom. I follow her. The swing of the bathroom door spills a ring of light into the dimly lit gym as two giggling girls pass us in their exit. Alexa pushes the door open, and we enter the bathroom. The walls are tiled with tiny pale-green squares; paint chips off the stalls; and half of the fluorescent light fixture pulses on and off in slow, shuddering lapses, casting us into bleached light, then shadow, then light again.

"Okay, so…" Alexa starts, sticking her face close to the mirror and wiping beneath her eyes for stray mascara. "In case you hadn't noticed, Eli's crushing on you."

"Oh…" I stumble, dismantled. Boys don't like me…that way. "I don't think so…"

She looks at me quickly, our eyes meeting in the mirror before she digs through her black Dickies bag and plucks out an eyeliner. She lines her eyes in thick, smoky violet, two sideways parentheses. "Oh, he does. But don't worry. It's just the way Eli gets…he gets crushes on *everyone*, so don't worry. It'll pass."

Like the flu.

"He used to like me too," she says, rolling her eyes. "Whatever." She pushes through the swinging doors again.

Is she mad at me? I don't want to come between her and Eli. If there's one thing being the new girl teaches, it's that you don't mess with the mounds of history that were here beforehand. That's dangerous. Best to keep under the radar.

I follow Alexa back to the snack table. Drew holds a cup of sweet-looking pink punch and talks to Tala about the play auditions yesterday.

Eli glares at Alexa, who shoots him a wide smile. She doesn't look mad.

Drew is trying to talk above the Bon Jovi playing. "I think the cast list will be up Monday. It's not like her to wait this long." He takes a tiny sip of punch. "This stuff tastes like battery acid." He takes another sip. "Want some?" He holds the cup out to me.

"I'm going to get some water," I tell them. "Is there a water fountain?" Tala points to the wall close to the door. I'm surprised Tala even knows where the fountain is. She never seems without her black Sigg bottle.

Behind me, I hear Eli say, "What the hell did you tell her?" but then I'm lost on the dance floor, which moves in small clusters of wriggling bodies. It is easy to cut through them to the fountain. I bend over it, the water cool against my lips.

Someone slams into me.

My face crashes into the fountain as water goes streaming down the front of my shirt. Pain surges through my face. My song journal tumbles to the floor. Fumbling, rattled, I look up, the dance a woozy, swirling rush around me. Feeling something wet down my front, I wipe my crushed nose. Sticky, not water. Blood.

The boy from English class looks back, his eyes wide with concern and embarrassment. He's holding a toppled ladder. The end of the sign he'd been hanging dips sadly on the ground, a large tear down its middle.

"Oh, jeez. I'm so sorry."

He scrambles to pick up my journal and hands it back to me. My father's picture has fluttered out, and he hands that back too. I stuff it quickly inside the pages, hoping I'm not getting blood all over it.

He takes in my face. "I'm so sorry. Oh, my god! You're bleeding. I wasn't watching…the ladder slipped…are you okay…I'm so sorry," he keeps repeating, struggling to right the ladder against the wall. He grabs a handful of napkins someone left on a chair. "Here."

I press the napkins to my bloody nose and clutch my journal to me. I nod, pointing to the ladder. "You know, you should get a license if you're going to be operating heavy machinery."

He laughs. "Yeah. That's funny."

We both know it isn't. I pull the napkins away and look at the dark-red blood.

"Jeez, that's bad."

"It's fine."

He jams his hands in his pockets. "So…you're in my English class."

"Yeah." I'm at a loss for words. Desperate, I morph into a parrot. "English class."

"Sam."

"Calle."

"Hi." We both look at anything but the other. My heart is beating ridiculously fast. I focus on the Cure's "Why Can't I Be You?" which is inducing a frenzy on the dance floor. My mom loves this song.

"Samuel!" Blond Girl from English flounces over beside him.

She wears a matching shell-pink halter top and miniskirt, strappy heeled sandals that I would break my neck in, and a diamond necklace that stands out against her smooth, tanned skin. I feel like a dump truck next to her.

"What happened? Oh. My. God. Did you *fall* off the ladder?" I have *never* understood girls like her, voices shrill and dramatic, speaking as if a ladder falling marks the twenty-third most tragic thing to happen in her life today. "The sign. It's ruined. The raffle starts in twenty minutes!" She shakes her head at the torn paper.

"The ladder slipped," Sam apologizes.

"This wouldn't happen if Kayla could *ever* finish anything on time!"

"I almost took Calle's head off."

"Who's Calle?" This girl has no power of deduction. I am, after all, the only other person directly involved at the moment.

"Me," I say lamely, muffled by napkin.

"Oh." She turns to Sam. "Samuel."

"Amber."

"Will you *please* help me tape this sign up? If Kayla couldn't manage to get it up *before* the dance at least we can get it up before the raffle." She sighs, studying the sign like a homicide detective at a murder scene. It's all very grim, this slaughtered sign. "We'll have to tape up the middle."

Sam smiles at her. He has slightly crooked Tom Cruise teeth, charming teeth that haven't been fixed into conformity by braces. So white. "Sorry about your face. It was nice meeting you, Calle."

"My nose thanks you." But he doesn't hear me.

Like a shadow, I walk back to the snack table where Eli has left half a plate of Oreos. He's gone, and so are the rest of them. I get more napkins for my nose and watch Sam tackle the ladder once again as Amber waves a roll of masking tape at him from below.

The music has shifted to OMD's "If You Leave," practically my mom's favorite song ever. Pulling my journal from my bag, I wipe a smudge of blood from one corner of my father's picture and make sure it is tucked securely inside. I find an empty chair in a corner as memory floods me: Mom crying at the end of *Pretty in Pink* when Andrew McCarthy chooses Molly Ringwald in the parking lot instead of the snotty rich girl he's supposed to be with. Through her tears, Mom telling me, "That's never happened. Nobody ever chooses me..."

CHAPTER 4
PERFECT BLUE BUILDINGS

...Mom plays Counting Crows all morning in the yellow light of the apartment. I am a shadow lingering about her. She looks through me, wanders the rooms. The curtains are drawn tight against a brown LA sky. Ted is late again, and Mom cries while she sings...

"SHE CAN'T PUT ICY HOT on her face, stupid."

Eli looks crushed. "Why not?"

"It will, like, burn her face off." Alexa snatches the tube away from him and shakes her head at me like he's a toddler who just keeps eating paste.

I spent the weekend nursing my cherry-tomato nose and raccoon bruises. I had hoped it would look better by Monday. No such luck.

"It looks bad, Cal." Eli pokes at my nose.

"Ow! It's fine if you don't touch it."

He sighs and offers to carry my backpack. Shaking my head, I watch down the hall where Sam hoists Amber's pile of books into his arms. She talks on her cell phone. Probably to someone at another locker.

Alexa follows my gaze. "Ugh, did he even apologize?"

"Sure. I mean, who doesn't apologize when they hit someone with a ladder?"

"Her." Alexa points a finger at Amber, who is now walking past us. She doesn't notice the other finger Alexa gives her.

"Hey, why did the blond girl die in the helicopter crash?" Eli doesn't wait for an answer. "She got cold and turned off the fan!"

Alexa laughs and, curling her arm around Eli's shoulders, walks with him toward the theater. I follow, watching them.

At every other school, I've always been too nerdy or too alone, a girl without a history. With the drama kids, it's different. They don't mind that I'm always writing in my song journal or listening to my headphones, don't care about my jeans and sweatshirt, my one-toned hair, my big bones. Eli has bleached the tips of his black hair white, and Drew has started wearing eyeliner and a crushed velvet cape. He chooses among three different cape colors, depending on his mood. I'm tame to these kids. For the first time, almost mainstream. A word said with amusement, and a little scorn, in this group. Weird. With them, I feel safer than you're supposed to feel in high school. I hope I don't screw it up.

They're well into rehearsals for the fall one-acts, three short plays by different playwrights. Alexa begged the drama teacher, Ms. Hecca, to let her do the entire set in black, white, and various shades of magenta, and has been frantically sketching designs for the past several weeks. Last night on the phone, she asked me to help paint the set, so I'm going to check it out. I've never really been into anything after school before. Maybe this will be different.

Drew is the lead in *The Actor's Nightmare,* and we're meeting him at rehearsal after school. We walk the path to the Little Theatre. The school has emptied at the final bell, students whirling away in cars and buses or on foot, a daily exodus off campus toward downtown, toward home, toward anywhere. Just away.

As much as I try to ignore it, my father's picture creeps back into my mind. Each day, at home, I check the cupboard for the cream-colored box. It's still there, where Mom thinks she's hiding it. At night, I look at his picture, the edges already filmy with my fingerprints. Online searches aren't helping. I don't know enough to find him. At school, though, I try to think about other things, not the man in the pea coat with the wind in his hair.

I take a deep breath as we near the theater. Eli and Alexa look so natural heading to drama rehearsal, discussing Alexa's weird German teacher (for some reason, there's a cot in her classroom), book bags casual over their shoulders. This is who they are, perfectly cast as high school drama kids. Everything around us is as it should be. The air, faintly stained with cold, is still warm in patches. I can hear the football team knocking into each other on the field that sprawls just beyond the main gym. I want to stop feeling like an extra in a movie who gets cut out of the picture in the final edit.

Up ahead, the Little Theatre squats in the central part of campus, dwarfed by the main gym and mini-gym nearby. The music building, which houses both music and the art department, peeks out from behind, the smallest of all four buildings. All of them were recently painted a thick-looking royal blue. Four perfect boxes in varying sizes, a nuclear blue-box family. The rest of the school buildings, the "academic" cluster, ignore the elective boxes; they sit solemn in their intellectually superior beige paint, peeling and scarred from past, painted-over graffiti.

"Hey, you guys." Drew waves at us from the door of the Little Theatre. He's in the red cape today: happy. "I've been waiting here for like an hour."

"Maybe you should stopping cutting seventh period," Eli jokes.

Ignoring him, Drew holds the thick, smoked-glass door open and we walk in. The interior reveals flat black walls and a smooth cement floor. A bunching of black curtains bookend the glass doors so that if they are pulled flush across the smoked glass, the room becomes a square black box. Rows of lights grip bars on the ceiling; it smells of dust and old makeup and, faintly, of pepperoni pizza. Students sit on the floor or on one of the two ripped couches slouching against the far wall. They stare at scripts, eat apples and SunChips, and drape their arms around one another.

My eyes try to take it all in at once.

Drew watches me absorb it. "It makes school bearable." He takes my arm and tows me toward one of the slouching couch groups. I see Tala eating chips in the midst of a faded orange couch. Tala, Drew tells me, is the assistant director.

"Hey, Tala. Calle's here. Where's Hecca?"

Tala looks up and smiles at me. "In the prop room. They're trying to squeeze Gaven into the old Hamlet costume for his scene with you."

"Good luck." He lets go of my arm, grabbing for some of Tala's corn chips.

Through the smoked glass of the theater door, I notice Amber walking alone toward the football field. She practically glides, her long legs the perfect length for her boot-cut jeans, the sunlight catching her hair. You'd think the girl had her own lighting designer.

Drew says, "Hey, can you show Calle what we need her to do?"

"So…you're in?" Tala asks.

I turn away from the window. "I'm in."

CHAPTER 5
CiRCLE

...in the thick tar night of Sacramento sky, with bats slipping like arrows across the stars, with Big Head Todd and the Monsters on so low I can barely hear them, I see Mom's car pull in, no Dan in the passenger seat, and I know he is gone like the others...I watch her open the car door, step outside, her face bathed in street lamp. Another one gone. She loves them so instantly, and with such hot light, and then it's like she just burns out—like the star we learned about in science that uses up all its fuel and just stops shining...

SOMETHING **SLAMS** INTO THE OTHER side of the gym lockers, the impact intense enough to rearrange the contents of my locker. One of my Doc Martens lands on my bare foot.

"Ow," I mutter, even though it doesn't really hurt. I hear footsteps run away at the sound of my voice. The locker room door bangs shut.

Still barefoot, I peer around the lockers. A girl is huddled on the floor, her brown hair draping her face. She wears only a white tank top, panties, and one green sock. Her hand gingerly pats her head.

I rush to kneel by her. "Are you okay?"

"Spanking," she says in a deep voice. She sits up, massaging the back of her head. "Damn, that hurts. Those bitches ambushed me."

I've never been one to swear. Not that I'm a prude or anything; it doesn't offend me. Sometimes, I swear in my head. It's just that when I try it out loud, I sound like an idiot. My mother laughs when I do it.

"You don't have the mouth for it," she's always told me. "You're no sailor, for sure."

This girl's a sailor. "Goddamn it," she says, looking around. "They took my goddamn clothes."

My face flushes at the next string of words (some of which I don't even recognize). Then she tucks her hair behind her ears, and I get the first good view of her face. Cass Gordon. Andreas Bay's loner girl. Notorious, she has no friends and spends more time cutting classes than going to them.

I can't believe anyone slammed Cass Gordon into a locker. She looks like she chews glass for breakfast. The first week of school, she beat up a senior. A senior *boy*.

"I have extra sweatpants in my locker. They kinda smell, but you can wear them." I look around for Ms. Davis. PE teachers have a strange way of disappearing just in time for us to be humiliated in the locker room.

Cass stares. "You're new."

"Yes." I stare back. "Do you want my sweatpants or not?" Brave. This girl could waste me.

Suddenly, like a July rainstorm, she smiles. It messes up her face, making it vaguely sweet. "Sure, new girl. I'll take the loaner."

I return to my open locker.

I hear her stand up. My navy-blue sweats are wadded into a ball and jammed into the back corner of my locker. When I pull them free; they feel cold and sort of damp. Gross.

"Never mind, new girl," I hear her say. Her arm appears around the corner, holding up a wad of clothing. "Dumped them in the garbage. Creative."

I wad the pants back up and return them to their dark corner. Shutting my locker, I slip on the new Docs my mom swears cost half her paycheck even though they were on sale. When I go around the corner to see Cass, she's gone.

• • •

I slip on my headphones to the strains of Counting Crows and walk the short path to the Little Theatre. An October mist curls around the few trees in the empty quad. The school is tired in the Friday air, hauled out and worked over a long week, only to be abandoned to the weekend.

I look forward to the theater on Fridays. We only have rehearsal officially on Tuesdays, Wednesdays, and Thursdays, but Alexa goes every day, so I do too. On Fridays, we paint flats in the square black room and talk about movies and music and teachers and Alexa's drawings. She outlines things, and I paint them in.

We sing along to Alexa's favorite singers, Kate Nash and Regina Spektor. And to one of my favorites, Jack Johnson. She doesn't laugh when I tell her that his music Band-Aids my soul. When I sing "No Good With Faces" for her, she tells me she loves my voice and that I should learn to play guitar.

Alone in the theater, we even talk about politics. She thinks the current president is ahead of his time compared to the former President who Alexa calls an anti-Aristotelian thinker because she's taking a philosophy elective now and knows something about Aristotle. We talk about movies. We both love director Cameron Crowe, and our favorite scene of all time is the "Tiny Dancer" scene in *Almost Famous* when they all sing on the bus. Because music always makes things better.

I sing loudly around Alexa.

As I head toward the royal-blue pod of buildings, I spot a lone figure walking, head down against the wind. Sam. Of English class and ladder tragedies. I cut across the circle of lawn toward him. He looks up. I smile, glad the bruises from our last encounter have long faded.

"Hi." I slide my headphones back.

"Your nose is all better."

"I'm a quick healer." Lame. It's been over a month.

He doesn't seem to notice. "What are you listening to?"

"Counting Crows." I bite my lip, not wanting him to think I listen to stupid music.

"I love their first disc."

"Oh, me too," I say. "'Omaha's one of my favorite songs of all times."

"That's a great one. It's on my iPod. So, where are you off to?"

I curl my hand tighter around my battered Walkman. "Little Theatre."

"Are you in the play?"

I shake my head. "Actually, I'm the assistant set designer." The title sounds unnecessarily important.

"Wow. That's really cool."

It isn't cool. Looking around, I notice that we're standing right in the center of the circle of grass. Gum and chip wrappers choke the edges of the lawn where it meets the cement.

He wears a letterman's jacket that looks different from the ones other guys wear.

"That's a nice jacket." I want to say important things to make him want to talk to me. But I also don't want to talk too much.

He glances down at it. "It was my grandpa's. He was a great football player."

"Are you?"

"Am I what?"

"A great football player."

He looks momentarily uncomfortable. "I'm okay." He pauses. "Our team's not so hot."

"So I gather." I wonder if I'm being coy or just obnoxious. I'm hoping for coy.

"You're a strange girl, Calle. I mean, you're not strange-weird, just strange-different, you know. I mean, no one I know talks like you." Has he even heard me talk that much? "You always say interesting things in English." I make a note to stop talking so much in English class. Interesting means weird.

"Hmm." I don't know what else to say. His hair curls in all different directions but manages to look ordered. He has sports-star-on-a-cereal-box hair. And wide boy shoulders.

"So, are you coming to the game?" He stuffs his hands into the back pockets of his jeans.

"What game?" I know what game he means and don't have the slightest idea why I just asked that. Coy again? I should stop. Coy doesn't work for me.

"The football game. The last one is tonight. JV starts at 5:30. I'm playing in it." He exchanges back pockets for jacket pockets. "You should come."

"Sure." Attempting to be casual, I give him what I hope is a charming, noncommittal smile. "I'll try."

The white of his smile shames toothpaste commercials. "Great. I'm number 21. My grandpa was 12, but he was a quarterback. I'm a running back. So I flipped his numbers."

I think this is supposed to be cool. He's waiting for me to say something about it, so I say, "That's so cool that you did that."

He nods, smiling. "Yeah, it's like a tribute to him. So you're coming? Look for me," he says with the confidence only popularity allows. "I'll see you there."

I frown, watching him stride across the quad. I don't know about this boy. This football-playing, perfect-smile, wide-shouldered boy. These are the kind of boys who shove smaller boys into trash cans. Last year, Henry—a kid in my art elective who drew amazing pictures of dragons—ended up in a PE locker for three hours after this kind of boy stuffed him in there. Why is this boy asking me to a football game?

CHAPTER 6
UNDERNEATH IT ALL

...Mom throws a last-minute Fourth of July barbecue, stringing Christmas lights behind the house all around the small patch of grass she calls our yard. People cram together, sipping beer or mineral water, talking over the No Doubt playing from the stereo in the window. Mom crouches by the tiny Weber, flipping hot dogs, and taking drags from the cigarette of the man in the Eagles shirt who has managed to attach himself to her. When he's not looking, she catches my eye and makes a hideous face until I dissolve into giggles in the corner...

"CAN YOU PUT A NEW CD on?" Alexa asks, blowing a stray lock of hair from her eyes. She is perched at the top of the ladder, painting a magenta trim across the top of the downstage flats.

I hop down from the stage, crossing to the chair where Alexa has propped Ms. Hecca's portable stereo. "Where's your rehearsal mix?" I ask, searching the ground nearby.

"It's not there?" she asks, brush poised. I shake my head. "Well, damn." She shrugs. "Must have left it at home. Ask Hecca if she has any music that doesn't suck."

I have Ben Harper and John Mayer in my bag, but Ms. Hecca offers me a Death Cab for Cutie disc, which I love. Hopefully, it doesn't fall into the "suck" category.

I start the disc going and reposition myself on the stage where I'm painting a piece of railing for a scene with Drew and Sara. "Cool," Alexa says, singing along. "My mom and I love this one," she says.

"My mom and I love it too," I tell her.

"What's she like?" She climbs down off the ladder to refill her paint tray.

"My mom?" I shrug. "She's pretty cool, I guess. Really pretty. Kinda flaky. Bothers me about my clothes."

Alexa laughs. "So she's a mom. What's your dad like?"

I hesitate, then say, "He left eight months after I was born. I've never met him."

Alexa pauses, her eyes evaluating me. Casually returning to the painting, she asks, "Have you ever tried to contact him?"

I shake my head. "I've asked my mom about him before, but she doesn't talk about him."

"Really? Not at all?"

I pull the wrapping off a new, thin paintbrush and rub the soft bristles across my palm. "She gets really weird when I bring him up, defensive. I guess he broke her heart."

Alexa sighs and surveys her work, maybe so she doesn't have to look at me. "That's so sad."

"He's a musician. I know that much. He left to try to make it with his band. I don't think my mom ever got over it."

Alexa frowns. "What about you?"

The picture is tucked away in my song journal. I almost tell her about finding it, but I stop. Shrugging, I say, "I have my mom."

"Stepdad?" Alexa climbs down from the ladder, eyebrows raised.

"A few." I dunk the paintbrush in the shiny black paint and watch it stream off back into the can.

"A few?" she repeats, moving the ladder to the next section of flat she has to paint.

"Four so far. My mom's been married four times, and we've lived with seven others. My mom says 'six' because Mark didn't count, but he ate all our food and left wet towels on the floor so I say he counts." Even though I'm not looking at her, I can feel her turn and stare.

"Seriously?" she asks.

I nod, my eyes fixed on painting a fake staircase. I know we're not normal. All the men. The moving. But that's just my mom.

"They're always Ted or Dan or Rob. See, my mom meets someone, and it's really great. And then we usually move and start a new life. And it's great for awhile. And then it's not. And then they leave. That's been pretty much it since kindergarten for me. At least that's when I really remember it clearly. I'm sure it's probably been that way my whole life."

"How many schools have you been in?" She starts to paint again, and I'm glad she's not still staring at me.

"Thirteen so far," I tell her. "No, fourteen counting this one."

"No way." She shakes her head, catching a drip with a wet cloth. "So you've had, like, no stability in your life at all."

I consider this. I don't think I know what she means. Stability. I've always had my mom. I tell her this. "And," I say, "they all drove Fords."

"Fords?"

I look up at her small frame on the ladder, her lips pursed in concentration. "You want the long version?" I ask.

She shrugs. "I'm not going anywhere. I have a lot of flats left to trim." She points down the row with her brush. "I mean, if you want to. I don't want to pry or anything."

"You're not," I tell her. And she's not. I've never talked to anyone this much about my mother's guys. Not even the counselor that the last school made me see because they thought I was suicidal when I wrote a poem about death for English class. We were reading Edgar Allan Poe—how could I *not* write about death? We moved the next week anyway, so it didn't even matter.

"Okay." I take a breath. Alexa watches me, waiting. "Four years after my dad split, she married Ted. Red Mustang. He's the first one I really remember. He didn't last long after we moved to L.A. He wanted to be a producer or director or something."

"That's original," Alexa says.

I tick our cities off on my fingers. "She took that one pretty hard. Then it was Chuck in Bakersfield with the Explorer. Art in Gilroy with the Freelander. Freeloader is more like it. And then Steve in Manteca with the Excursion. That guy had a whole separate family in another city. Total loser. Then we went to Sedona,

Arizona, for a brief new-age period my mom went through when I was nine."

"Another Ford?"

I nod. "Yeah. Tom. Two-toned Maverick. He left us in the middle of the night, and a week later we moved to Santa Barbara where my mom knew a guy."

"Santa Barbara's nice," Alexa offers, moving her ladder again.

"It was okay. I went to, like, three different schools there, depending on who Mom was with. But then Dan 'Call me Dad—it's just one letter away' showed up and moved us to Sacramento. Gray Ford Taurus. He lasted the longest of any of them. They even had a real wedding with flowers and food and stuff. My mom wouldn't get out of bed for three days after he left."

"That sucks."

"I ate a lot of cereal during those three days." I stop, thinking about the week following Dan's exit. Living in the U-Haul. Eating Burger King because a friend of Mom's worked there. I don't tell Alexa this part. "Then we met Ted Number 2. He had this battered, lemon-yellow Ford truck with a bench seat. He was blond, tan, a total surfer guy—younger than my mom."

"Sounds cute," Alexa says, taking a break from her painting to stretch her arms and back.

"Very cute," I nod. "He was going to San Diego to design surfboards, so we went with him. We were three blocks from the beach in this tiny house. We ate pizza a lot and listened to the Stones, Cat Stevens—he had great taste in music. Drew would say it sucks, but it doesn't. When Ted Number 2 moved to Hawaii without us, I told Mom she should never trust a guy in a Ford ever again."

"At the least," Alexa agrees, watching as I finish up the railing. "And now you're here."

"Rob. Silver-blue Ford Focus."

Alexa snorts. "Your mom has a slow learning curve."

"Yeah," I sigh, placing the paint top back on the can. I think back to that night in the small kitchen in San Diego. Mom's penny landing on Andreas Bay. She was so eager to leave, anxious and flighty. I wanted to stay in San Diego, but Rob thought it was important for us to get a clean start. I told him none of our starts had ever been clean.

• • •

I slip on my headphones and pay three dollars to get into the game. I am convinced that headphones give me an immediate excuse for not being with someone. If not, at least they make me look less lame for being alone. This is what I tell myself, though I don't totally believe it. Ben Harper will have to be my date for the evening. His rendition of Maya Angelou's "Still I Rise" floods my ears, a strange musical backdrop to the rough, gritty game before me.

I have actually never been to a football game and am surprised by the energy around me. The air seems smoky in the translucent evening, lit by the field lights that look like transmitters for alien communication. Andreas Bay sweatshirts dot the metal stands to the right, splashes of bright blue and green. The other school's colors are red and white, and their fan-filled bleachers to the left look bloodstained.

A rail-thin girl sneaks in under a curl in the chain-link fence to the side of the visitors' stand. Cass Gordon. She doesn't show up to school, but she comes to a football game? She climbs to the top of the bleachers and parks herself in the middle, a dot of black among the red shirts.

I look back at Cass, who has no awkwardness with being alone. With my life, you'd think I'd be a pro, but I'm not. I don't know whether to sit down in the bleachers or hang out on the dirt track that circles the field like a drained moat. I don't see any students watching the game; most just seem to be milling about in clumps, like they would at a dance or a party. None of the clumps are familiar, so I opt for the snack shack. I'm hungry anyway, and it will give me something to do.

A girl from my Spanish class is working behind the counter. She's the nice, student council type, so full of school spirit that I imagine she has to be drained once a week or she'll pop. I slip off my headphones.

"Hi, Calle!"

And she knows *everyone's* name.

"Hey…" I, however, do not.

"I'm Kayla. From Spanish." It seems like half the girls in the freshman class are named Kayla.

"Hi." On the chalkboard behind the counter, someone has drawn pictures of hot dogs and sodas and candy bars in a crooked border. "Can I get nachos and a Pepsi?"

"Absolutely!" Kayla will end up as a cruise director. She rushes to the back counter and dips a paper tray into a glass container of chips. Standing on her tiptoes, she leans onto the pump that oozes the orange cheese onto the chips.

"Do you want peppers?" she asks over her shoulder.

"No, thanks." My mother is on such a health kick lately that she'd have a heart attack if she saw me eat this fluorescent goo. I hand Kayla three dollars. The can of Pepsi is cold and wet from the cooler. A piece of ice rolls around the rim.

I sit near the bottom of the home bleachers and eat half the nachos before they congeal. An announcer's voice fills the air.

"Stevens is down on the thirty yard line. Second and seven."

Whatever that means. I search for Sam's jersey. He's on the field, Number 21. He looks like an upside-down triangle with his huge shoulder pads and narrow waist.

He breaks from a pack of jerseys and runs toward the end of the field. People around me jump to their feet, cheering.

"Touchdown. Sam Atkins!" The announcer's voice says his name as one looping cry.

The people around me high-five and yell through cupped hands. Their energy warms me. I smile and watch Sam. His teammates surround him, smacking him on the helmet and shoulders, which looks like it hurts, but he doesn't seem to mind.

"They haven't won a game all year."

I'm not totally sure the woman next to me is talking to me, but she doesn't seem to be sitting with anyone. She is old, maybe seventy, and her skin is ashes and coal. But I mostly notice how tiny she is. If it weren't for her thick gray hair, I would take her for a small child at first glance.

"Hmm?"

She looks at me from under thin gray lashes. Her eyes are the color of blue Kool-Aid, and they stand out against her dark face, deep and liquid. They are too young in her mass of gray-black wrinkles.

"They haven't won a game all year," she repeats. "Can I have a nacho?" She points at my half-eaten nachos tray sitting between us.

"Sure. You can have them all."

She picks up the tray and balances it on her small, blanketed lap. Pulling a soggy chip from the coagulated mass of cheese, she pops it in her mouth and licks her fingers.

"Yummy."

"Not bad for toxic waste."

She lets out a deep laugh that shakes her whole body. The nachos nearly slide right off her lap. The laugh passes as quickly as it escaped.

"I'm Emily Martin," she extends her small hand.

I shake it. "Calle."

She looks back out over the field. "Who are you here for?" She extracts another goopy nacho and points it vaguely at the field.

I flush. "No one really. I mean, Sam Atkins invited me."

She raises her eyebrows. Or at least I think she raises her eyebrows. She doesn't actually have any eyebrows, just brow bones. The skin there seems to rise, and her forehead skin wrinkles.

"He's a good ballplayer, that Sam. His grandfather...whew," she lets out a puff of air and downs another nacho. "Now there was a great football player." She licks some cheese from her fingers.

"You knew Sam's grandpa?"

She nods. "Tom Atkins, Senior. But he didn't take his scholarship. Stayed on at the grocery." When I shrug, she adds, "The Atkins family owns Bay View Foods."

"I'm new to Andreas Bay." Bay View Foods is the main supermarket in Andreas Bay, except for the Safeway. But most of the locals shop at Bay View. Safeway's for traitors who don't buy local.

"Ah. I thought you were." She sets the empty nachos tray between us and pats my leg. "The Atkinses have been in Andreas Bay since it was founded in 1892. Sad story, that family." She frowns and looks out over the field. "Listen to me. Gossiping about things nobody really knows. Still, if it hadn't been for that Gordon girl…"

"You mean Cass?"

Before she can answer, another cry goes up from our section, and I realize the game is over. We've won for the first time this year. People pour out of the stands, and I am swept away by their movement, finding myself suddenly standing on the dirt track near the field, my nachos plate, my soda, and strange, tiny Emily somewhere behind me.

I look for her, but the crowd has condensed at the bottom of the stands and on the track, a sudden pack of sardines marinating in this rare victory. I study the visitor stands. Cass is no longer clumped in the middle.

Scanning the crowd, my eyes lock with Sam's. His hair is messy from his helmet, and he has two thick black streaks under his eyes. He sees me, smiles, and mouths, "Thanks for coming."

"You're welcome," I mouth back, a warm chill spreading through my body like bathwater as he's swallowed up by the crowd.

• • •

My mother has become a vegetarian. It truly sinks in the Saturday after the football game when I wake up and discover our refrigerator full of soy dogs, tofu patties, and Rice Dream.

"Mom!"

"Yeah, sweetie?" Her voice emerges from the office-exercise room. She has Fleetwood Mac on, and Stevie Nicks sings "Gypsy." I can hear my mother singing along, her voice high and airy—not like Stevie's at all.

"Where's the milk?"

She comes out of the room dressed in cobalt-blue yoga pants and a tight black T-shirt; she has a hand towel draped around her neck.

"I bought Rice Dream. It's the same thing."

No. It really isn't.

"Umm. I like regular low-fat milk. And Golden Grahams."

I check the cupboard. There are no Golden Grahams. I look at her. Wait for an explanation.

She bites her lip and mops her forehead with the towel.

"Golden Grahams are full of refined sugar, honey. They aren't good for you."

Refined sugar? It's happening again.

"Mother." She knows she is in trouble when I call her that. "We've lived here barely two months, and you're already totally different."

"Calle Lynn, that is not fair and not true." I'm always 'Calle Lynn' when she is 'Mother.'

With each new move, my mom gives her life a makeover. Which was fine before. It never changed my stuff really. But this is too much.

"Mother," I say again. "In Los Angeles, it was facials, Pilates, and California cuisine. In Sedona, we communed with the energy of the vortex, and we hung crystals all over the house. In Sacramento, you developed an intense fascination with floral arrangements and color-coordinated furnishings.

"In San Diego, you surfed…no, you *bought* a surfboard and bleached your hair. You wore flip-flops to work. Now, you're a vegetarian yogi, Mother. Which is fine—it's fine. For you. I just want to wake up and have milk and Golden Grahams."

I hear Rob come through the front door. He enters the kitchen, sweaty from a run. He stops, glancing back and forth between my mother and me. "What?"

I sigh. "Your wife is now a vegetarian. Look in the fridge."

He does and then looks at my mom.

"Alyson?" Rob has a way of asking a question with almost every word he speaks. He often only speaks in one or two words. Very economical.

"So now I'm on trial for wanting to live a healthy lifestyle?" In every argument, my mother makes herself into the defendant. Maybe she should go to law school. Or stop watching those ridiculous court shows on TV.

"No trial." Rob picks up a container of tofu from the top shelf and shakes it. It slides around in translucent-looking goo. He wrinkles his nose, replaces the container, and closes the refrigerator door. "No hamburger?"

"Red meat is horrible for you. Kelly at work gave me an article… it was horrible. You should read it." Her eyes fill with tears. "I'm just trying to do what's best for us as a family."

Now I look like a jerk because I'm making a big deal out of this. It's not like she's murdered the old couple next door or something. She's just…she's just *her*. She *always* does this.

"Maybe we could also get regular milk? You can buy the organic kind. And normal cereal. No granola!"

She nods and puts her arms around me, smelling of jasmine oil. That's something about my mom that never changes. She has always smelled like jasmine.

• • •

"Hey, Mr. Tambourine Man, play a song for me…

Sitting bolt upright in my bed, I wait for the strains of the song to drain from me as the moonlit room replaces my dream. I pick up my clock so I can read it. I always place the bright green numbers face down on my nightstand or I can't sleep. I look at it. 4:30 a.m. And it's almost Monday. My alarm will go off for school in under three hours.

I shake my head and stare out the window. The moon, smug in the night sky, stares back. It's been awhile since I dreamed about my Tambourine Man. Once I asked my mother about the song. I was twelve, and we were eating pancakes at an IHOP just off the I-5. I remember that she looked at me strangely, her eyes dark.

"I hate the Byrds," she said. "Eat your pancakes."

I don't ask her anymore.

The song is gone now, but my heart still pounds. Something is seriously wrong with me. Sam said I am a strange girl. Those were his words. Strange. Girl. I scan my bookshelf. In the green glow of the clock I hold like a flashlight, I see Jane Austen, Stephen King, Toni Morrison, and J. R. R. Tolkien cohabiting.

A teddy bear Red Mustang Ted gave me is stuffed between a book of world poetry I never read and a dictionary with all the Xs next to the words I look up. My CDs form flat plastic rows along the top shelf. I pause, my eyes on my music.

I listen to strange music.

I listen to my mother's music. She loves Tom Petty and Bruce Springsteen and Alicia Keys, and I breathe it in through her. Some of it's mine, but my mom always seems to make it hers. She likes Taylor Swift a lot more than I do, even though I'm the one who bought the CD. And just last week, she took my Ingrid Michaelson disc and hasn't given it back.

A girl in San Diego once told me that I like all the music her thirty-six-year-old brother likes. She wasn't mean about it or anything; she just thought it was interesting that I didn't listen to the same music as other kids did. And I don't have an iPod or a cell phone. I have a *Walkman*. No one buys CDs anymore. And I don't know any of the latest bands. Don't know about podcasting or how to text message someone. No Facebook (Mom would freak!).

I'm strange.

I push the covers aside and walk silently to the front door, the dream already lost, my heart slow and rhythmic. I can hear Rob snoring, little putters that sound like a distant moped. I open the door and pad out in my socks to the edge of the street where I can just make out a thin band of the sea, still dark, even in the light of the moon. A strip of aluminum in the night. My socks are soon soaked.

My mother had me when she had just turned nineteen, which never seemed that unusual. But Alexa's mom is forty-eight and Drew's parents are over fifty. My mom was five years older than I am now when she had me. Maybe she and my dad met at a club where she was working. He was older, playing in a band. Maybe he wrote a song just for her.

My mom keeps two pictures in a side-by-side silver frame. In the first, she is pregnant with me. Her hair is dark, and she wears a man's white T-shirt over her round belly. Maybe my father's shirt. In the picture, she's looking away and laughing, her hand settled over her belly, her dark hair spilling over her shoulders. The other picture is me three months old, round-faced and blinking after a bath, a towel draped over my head.

I never thought until now that my father must have taken those pictures. Said something to make her laugh. Dried me off after the bath with a blue-edged towel. And then he left, and my mom and I began our Ford tour of California. We had each other. And we had our music. Her music.

Sam said "strange girl." Standing there in the chill, the sea air pawing its way into my hair, I know it's my mother who makes me strange.

CHAPTER 7
ISLAND IN THE SUN

Mom storms out, door slamming...I should've known better than to ask about what happened with Dan, should've known she'd freak out. Needing to dream, hide, I play Weezer full blast; she's no longer home to tell me to turn it down. The sky through my window is white sand. A bird sits on the sill; if I invite him in, I won't be so alone...

TABITHA DALY'S TWO LOW PIGTAILS stick out like handlebars. When she talks, they ticktock back and forth, a hypnotic clock. It distracts me, so I am not totally listening to her.

"Calle?"

"Hmm?"

"What symbol should we do for our society?"

Somehow I have ended up with a cool group for our English project. Sam's in my group, much to Amber's annoyance. I laughed when she got stuck with Caleb Wilkins. He doesn't do anything but pick his nose and draw Lara Croft, Tomb Raider, in compromising positions on his plastic binder cover. Trey Carter is also in my group. He's really funny but takes school seriously, so he won't just expect the rest of us to do all the work. And Tabitha knows *everything*. She's like the person version of Trivial Pursuit.

I'm lucky. A cool group and a cool project, as far as school stuff goes. Mr. Ericson wants us to "draw and analyze a symbol for our society." We are going to be reading the novel *Animal Farm*. But first we're going to analyze our own society on a symbolic level. We don't know how to do it, but it seems like a cool project.

"Are we just going to look at the United States?" I ask. "Or more globally?"

Sam speaks up, something he never does in class. "We should focus on the United States as an island. Wait. Is an island a symbol?" He looks embarrassed.

Tabitha looks surprised. Sam's a jock. Tabitha and her friends think that group has the IQ of a shoulder pad. I glance at his flushed cheeks. Maybe the jock image is just a cover. After all, it doesn't always pay to be the smart kid in high school. Only so many of the smart kids get to hang on the fringes of popularity in the semi-popular student-council, honors classes crowd. And Tabitha and her friends have that market cornered.

"It could be," she nods. "Do you mean in the way the United States isolates itself in its own gluttony?"

He shrugs. "It was just an idea." The confidence I'm used to seeing in him seems to be hiding out in the letterman jacket slung over the back of his chair.

Trey leans forward. "No. It's a good idea."

51

I nod at him. "Really good. A lot of potential."

There's that Colgate smile. Like the sun. I remember what Emily said at the game. What's sad about his family?

Tabitha sits straight up. "Hey. We could draw a big picture of the country as an island, separated from the rest of the world by its own corporate control systems—McDonald's and Starbucks and Gap. We could play music clips to support our ideas."

Trey starts to sketch a cartoon-like picture of the United States adrift in a choppy sea.

"Wow, Trey." Sam peers over his shoulder at the Gap model emerging like a weed from the soil of the island.

The bell rings. Sam stands, collecting his binder. Amber is by his side before the bell finishes ringing. He gives a wave as she curls her arm through his and pulls him toward the door. At the door, he turns back to us.

"Maybe we should meet after school one day this week to pull it all together, like Thursday or something?"

Tabitha agrees for all of us.

Feeling my face flush, I gather up my binder and Walkman and meet Drew at the door, hoping he doesn't notice my red face.

CHAPTER 8
ANOTHER FIRST KISS

...the dock of the boardwalk is screaming with summer people in shorts and burned noses; my mother eats a caramel apple and smiles big and sloppy at me. A faraway radio plays They Might Be Giants as two people embrace on the curved moon of green grass near the boardwalk edge. Seeing them, my mother stops smiling and tosses the half eaten apple in a garbage can...

"I'M GOING TO BE LATE today," I tell my mom. "I'm meeting a friend."

"No set painting?" she asks, stretching out on the floor of the kitchen in her yoga tights.

"Alexa's out of town for the weekend with her parents." I slurp cereal from my duck bowl and watch my mom bend her head to her knee.

"That's nice," she says, muffled. "I'm glad you're making friends."

My eyes stray to the cabinet where I found my father's picture. "Mom?"

"Hmm?"

"Do you ever wonder where Dad is?"

She stops stretching and looks up at me. "He's at work."

"Not Rob. Dad. My father."

I look at the soggy remains of my cereal in the bottom of the bowl, waiting. Outside, the fog is starting to thin, and I can just make out the tall eucalyptus tree in the neighbor's yard.

She stands and grabs the towel she'd been sitting on.

"No, I don't," she says as she leaves the room. I rinse my duck bowl and go to school.

• • •

This afternoon the theater is dark inside, the set a strange ghost in shadows, sitting ready for opening weekend on Friday. Rehearsal's not until five tonight. I wait for Sam outside, clutching our class poster. He missed class today, so I told him I'd show him our project.

"So let's see the goods." Sam walks up beside me, his backpack slung over his left shoulder. I unroll the picture and show him, pointing to the green A in the circle.

"Sweet," he says, his eyes scanning Mr. Ericson's response. "I don't think I've ever had a perfect score on anything before. Good thing I got into a smart group."

"You're smart," I say, taking the paper back and rolling it into a tube.

He shrugs. We stand for a moment in silence, waiting. It seems stupid now that we met here. I could have read him the comments over the phone.

"Do you have to go?"

SONGS FOR A TEENAGE NOMAD

"No," I say quickly.

"Do you want to go for a walk or something?" Sam has a way of looking past my shoulder when he talks to me. Like he's looking for someone. Maybe he doesn't want people to see us talking. I feel nervous and strange in my sweatshirt, my baggy jeans.

I say, "What about Amber?"

I don't really care about Amber, but it seems like something to say. She's always hanging on him after class or passing him tiny notes folded into triangles branded with pink penned hearts and smiling faces.

"Amber and I don't go out," he says, this time looking at me, eyebrows raised. "We're not together anymore. Besides, it's just a walk. I'm not getting us a room."

"I know." I falter and look at my feet. They seem big in my shoes, clunky like battleships attached to the ends of my legs. Amber wears shoes that make her three inches taller and seem a part of her long, tan legs. Her lipstick matches her pink plastic sandals.

We don't talk on the way out to the beach. Our feet move in time with each other, and I'm aware of the way he waits a little for me, slowing his natural pace. He's wearing his grandfather's letterman jacket; the wool is old and soft. Light hangs around the edge of his profile, a force field. I'm a girl with old sweatshirts and battleship feet and no lipstick at all. He is too cute to be walking with me.

"I really admire you, Calle," he says, finally.

We stop at a rim of hardened sand that crumbles slowly onto the powdery beach. Tiny tufts of grass hang around, and there are shells, cracked and bleached white with sun. The sky is a thin color-less blue. I find it hard to believe that he would admire me. I feel plain and bulky and wrong in the salt air that breathes around us.

"Oh?" I don't want to say something stupid, so I try not to say much.

He looks out at the sea. "You're so smart, and you don't care what other people think of you."

"I care." *I care very much what you think of me*, I want to say to him but don't.

He sits down and motions for me to sit next to him, our legs dangling from the lip of sand. My stomach churns with nerves.

"What I mean is you're not that stupid, manufactured pretty that the other girls are…you're just your own pretty. You're just you." He looks at me sideways. "I admire that."

"I'm not pretty." I look straight ahead at the waves. The conversation seems unreal, something that should be happening to another girl. A girl on TV. Not to me.

"You're pretty. And smart. And just…not like everyone else."

I'm strange. I get it. We've established that.

"What's your mom like?" he asks.

What a weird question to ask me. "She's okay," I say. "Very pretty and funny." And not at all like me. "She makes some dumb choices in men, moves us around a lot. But she's doing her best, I guess."

"So you're close." He looks a little sad for a moment. He kicks at the sand with his heel and stares at the ocean.

"We sort of have to be," I tell him. "It's just us. I don't have anyone else."

"Dad?"

I tell him about my father.

"Do you ever wonder about him?" He moves his hand to cover mine; it's warm like the sun on my face.

"One time," I find myself telling him, "I found a newspaper clipping about his band."

"He's in a band?"

I nod, watching the light hit the water, sending small sprays of diamonds across the waves. "He's a musician. Plays in a band called 'Wonderland'—at least he used to. I found the clipping in one of my mom's books."

"Did you ask her about it?"

"She wouldn't say much. Just that she didn't know if he was still playing. She took the article. We don't talk about it. You know the funny thing is, until recently, I didn't really think much of him. He was just…" I search for the right word. "He wasn't real. Like a character from a movie you don't notice. Like someone at another table in the restaurant where the main character is eating."

Acutely aware of his hand on mine, I tell him the story. Our moves. My different schools. The Fords.

"How do you even deal with it?"

I watch a gull dive at the water and come up empty. "It's just what we do. There's this Indigo Girls song called 'Leaving.' Have you heard it?" He shakes his head. "In the song, the singer basically says that leaving is the only thing she knows how to do. That's like us. It's what we know."

He nods. "I've lived here my whole life. Sometimes I wish I could just start over in a new place, a new life."

"It has its benefits," I tell him, looking out at the water, the sand, the calling gulls—the landscape of his whole life. The subject of my father seems closed. I'm relieved. How can I explain something that feels so uncertain, like sand slipping through my fingers?

"What about all your friends?" he asks. His hand is growing hot; it's distracting me, dismantling me. I try to concentrate on his words as they come to me, but the air in my chest is tight.

"I have my journal and my headphones." I laugh a little, a forced, nervous laugh, thinking of our hands, of the information I've so easily given him.

"A boyfriend?" He stops kicking the sand and looks closely at me. A real laugh now. "Hardly."

He looks surprised. "What about Eli? I always see you with him at school."

I'm amazed that he notices me at school. "Nope," I say. "Eli's just a friend."

"You listen to that CD player a lot."

"It's a way to pass the time, you know." I don't tell him that it's so much more than that, the record of my days.

"If you're so into music, you should get an iPod."

Without thinking, I say, "We can't really afford one." Not wanting him to think we're poor or something, I rush on. "Besides, my mom's ex-boyfriend Ted gave me this. It's the only thing I have of his."

He nods. "So it's special."

"Yeah." I give myself a mental kick for the 'can't afford it' comment. So not cool.

"Who's your favorite band?"

I shrug. "Don't have one. My music taste is kind of all over the place. I like a lot of '90s stuff, older than that even. I like a song if I can hear it again years later and still like it."

"Me too," he says. "But we've got to get some newer stuff on your playlist. Some Katy Perry or the Black Eyed Peas at least."

My heart stirs. "Okay."

We sit for a minute and soak in the sounds of the beach. I don't tell him about "Tambourine Man" even though it's tapping against the back of my mind, anxious to be shared. Then Sam takes his hand away, digs into his backpack, and produces a bottle of water.

"Thirsty?"

I shake my head. He takes a long drink. My hand feels light, like it could float away.

"Actually, yes." I reach for the bottle and take a drink, wanting something to put my hand around. When my lips touch the rim, I realize that he just drank from it, that his mouth was here.

Before I can hand the bottle back, he leans into me. His kiss is water and salt and sun, and I only wish that there were music, so that someday I'll remember this when I hear it play.

CHAPTER 9
YELLOW

In the pewter light of early morning, my mother croons along to Coldplay on the radio, her knees propped up against the steering wheel of the parked moving van. She eats powdered donuts from a white box, and the sugar sifts down on her chest like snow. I wonder how she can sing so loud when she's spent all night crying over another man...

SAM WEARS A YELLOW SHIRT that deepens his olive skin. Today I see that shirt everywhere. I watched the yellow shirt getting hot chocolate from the cafeteria window this morning. I saw the yellow shirt at break, lounging on the bench across from the boys' bathroom with Jake Simon and Ray Herrara.

Now the yellow shirt sits in the library bent over a book. I finish making a photocopy of the *New Yorker* article I'm using for my English paper and return the magazine to the front desk.

"Hey, Calle." Sam spots me.

I slide into the chair across from him.

"Hey." My face is warm from the heat he seems to give off. All I can think of is that kiss yesterday at the beach. I want to seem relaxed, casual. I hope my face isn't the neon sign it feels like, flashing, *"You kissed me…you kissed me…you kissed me."*

"Working away your lunch?" He nods at the article in front of me on the table.

"You too. Isn't there actually a rule about football players in the library?"

"Ouch." He smiles and cups a hand under his chin. "I have a math test next period. Treveli's class."

"Known for the tests from the seventh level of hell."

He taps his pencil on the open page and makes a face. "Quadratic formula. Very essential information to my life."

I would never reveal in a million years that I actually find the quadratic formula somewhat interesting. "No kidding."

"So, are you coming over this afternoon?"

"Am I still invited?"

"Of course."

He looks over his shoulder at the sound of people entering the library. Chela Walters, one of Amber's friends, walks through the door with her usual pack of friends. They look straight off the cover of *CosmoGirl*.

Sam's smile disappears. "Treveli said that we could come early for help if we wanted it." He starts gathering up his books. "I'll see you later, okay? Four o'clock?"

"Oh, okay." I sit up straighter. "Yeah. Four." I watch him hurry out of the library, nodding to Chela and then pushing through the heavy glass doors.

Outside, I see the yellow shirt heading nowhere near Mr. Treveli's classroom.

. . .

I turn my key in the lock, annoyed that I even have to make this stop at home. At lunch today, Eli had the brilliant idea that he could balance a hot dog (complete with bun, mustard, and relish) on the end of his nose. Back arched so that his nose pointed skyward, he balanced that stupid hot dog for three minutes and forty-six seconds before he sneezed and sent the hot dog all over me—and my white shirt.

So I'm home to change before heading over to Sam's.

I push open the door but stop when I hear my mom's voice. What's she doing home from work so early? At first I think she's talking to herself, but I soon realize that she's on the phone. I start to call to her, but something in her tone stops me. Still in the open doorway, I tip my head, listening.

"Well, then where is he now?" Her voice is tight, irritated. "Uh-huh…but I thought he had another year?"

I take a few steps forward into the entryway. Silence. She must be listening to the person on the other end of the phone.

The door blows shut behind me. I jump. Mom hurries into the entry, the portable phone attached to her ear. She's wearing a Jack Johnson T-shirt and a pair of Rob's pajama bottoms.

"I'll call you back," she says quickly and clicks off the phone.

"Hi, Mom!" I say too brightly.

"I thought you were meeting a friend?" She tries to smile but looks more nervous than anything else.

"I thought you were at work."

"I got off early," she says. Then she notices my shirt. "What happened to you?"

"Eli spilled a hot dog on me. I have to change." We eye each other for a minute. "Who was that?" I nod at the phone.

She looks at it as if she's never seen it before. "Oh, no one. Kelly from work. We were just gossiping. About a guy we work with."

"Jason?" I ask. My mom works with a guy named Jason who just left his wife for some waitress from Denny's. I've been hearing about it all week.

She looks guilty. "Yeah. Jason. Kelly's at work and just wanted to call and chat a bit."

I smile at her. "Jeez, and you think Alexa and I are gossip monkeys."

I walk by her to my room. After slipping into a new black shirt that my mom bought me last weekend, I find her still in the entry. She is biting her lip, staring at the floor.

"Mom?" I pick up my backpack.

She starts. "Oh! Yeah?"

"Are you okay?"

She smiles. "Sure. Sure. Just spacing out." She gives a little wave and disappears into the kitchen.

Downtown, I walk by OM!, the store my mom works in. I stop and stare in the window. Jason leans on the counter, flipping the pages of a magazine, bored. He is bobbing his head to music I can't hear. My mom's conversation tugs at me. I thought Kelly was working today.

• • •

I knock on Sam's door at 4:03, having waited down at the bottom of the driveway for more than ten minutes so that I don't seem too eager. The house is a tall, white Victorian with a wide black driveway. In the front yard, a tree with yellow leaves bends like a dancer. I take a few breaths.

No one answers, so I ring the doorbell, unleashing a tumbling string of moaning notes. A haunted-house doorbell. Still no answer. I check the address again, 638 Shore View. Iron numbers bolted into the frame of the white porch. I check my watch again. 4:04. From the front step, I can see the ocean, a strip of sheet metal between the autumn-colored trees, silver and then yellow and red. Money buys views like this. Money and luck. I ring the doorbell again and memorize the view.

Sam appears at the door looking flustered and tired, like he's been sleeping. In jeans and sock feet, he pulls the door behind him and steps out onto the front porch with me.

"Hi," he says. His hair looks like he has been running his hands through it for hours.

"Are you okay?" His eyes seem red. Crying?

"Umm. Not really." He steps lightly from foot to foot; the cold of the stoop must eat socks in seconds.

"What's wrong?"

"No big deal. Some family stuff is all. But would you be pissed if I had to cancel today?"

"No," I say. Disappointed, yes. Not pissed. "It happens. Anything I can do?"

"No. No. I just have to go. I'm sorry, Calle. We'll talk tomorrow at school, okay?" Without waiting for an answer, he ducks back inside.

. . .

We don't talk at school the rest of the week.

In English, he is a gunshot out the door. I don't try to catch up with him. Now, I'm pissed.

On Friday, I watch Sam race away, and Drew raises his eyebrows. "Something you want to tell me, Cal?"

I scoop up my folder and jam it into my backpack. "No. Why?"

"No sudden interest in football you'd like to discuss?"

I glare at him. "What, Drew?"

He holds up his hands in defense. "No implications. Just wondering." He walks out with me, fiddling with the hem of his "I love mullets" T-shirt.

Eli joins us in the hallway, linking his arm through mine. He wears shiny red pleather pants. He says, "You ready for tonight?"

Tonight is opening night of the fall festival one-acts. "Of course."

"So," Eli begins, "a bear walks into a bar and says, 'I'd like a gin and...'" He takes a long pause and then says, "'Tonic.' The bartender says, 'What's with the pause?' The bear holds up his paws and says, 'Well...I'm a bear.'" Eli cracks up.

Drew looks at him sideways. "What?"

"Get it?" Eli frowns. "Paws. Pause. Oh, never mind...umpf." A girl runs into Eli head on.

Cass Gordon doesn't apologize. She looks straight at me, her eyes penetrating the fence of hair that falls in front of her face.

"Whoa. Sorry for driving in your lane," Eli jokes.

I try to smile at her, but before I can, she plows away down the hall, mowing over several other people like a street-cleaning machine.

Eli watches her, fascinated. "That is one weird chick."

• • •

At first, I think my eyes are lying, melding together the people I
have on my mind and standing them together like toy soldiers.
I turn the volume down on the Black Eyed Peas blaring into my
ears, but my eyes aren't lying. They stand pressed into the narrow
alleyway created by the foreign language portables.

Sam and Cass. In a conspiratorial huddle, tipping heads toward
each other, whispering, her hand clutching a chunk of his jacket,
rooting him there like the mooring of a boat.

I'm glad they don't see me. Their huddle is a secretive loop of her
clutch and his tilting, nodding head. I step away from the building
and head toward my Spanish class across the way from their alley. I
cannot even begin to imagine how they know each other: Sam, one
of the visible, glowing gems of the campus who knows this place
is his turf, and Cass, like a scab on flawless skin, so horribly and
embarrassingly not a part of this place.

They shouldn't even cross paths, but their talking—her hand on
him like they *know* each other—sends me spinning, jostled like a
pack of gum slipping to the bottom of a grocery sack. What could
they possibly be talking about?

• • •

I sit in my plastic Spanish class seat, my CD player a marsupial
in the pouch of my sweatshirt, wishing I were at the beach and
not here at school where everything seems to slide farther from
normalcy each day.

• • •

The theater hums with a full closing-night house who wait in papery light for the start of the play. I am backstage with a headset that lets me talk to the small lighting booth at the back of the Little Theatre. Alexa is calling the show from the booth. I have been promoted to assistant stage manager backstage because the girl who was supposed to do it switched to home schooling.

I peek out through the black curtains even though Ms. Hecca told me not to. "If you can see the audience," she said, "the audience can see you."

I look anyway, watching the shuffling of green programs that have my name under "crew" and smelling the chocolate-chip cookies Sara's mom baked for the show to sell at intermission.

"Calle?" Alexa's voice comes over the headset.

"Yeah?" I click back.

"Five minutes."

I go tell the actors, who smile widely. Sara blows me a kiss from under a messy blond wig. Drew gives me a thumbs-up and pulls a pair of black pants over boxers with hearts on them. He spends most of the play in those boxers and has started wearing them around backstage for luck before putting on the pants he wears in the first scene. His legs are the color of bleached driftwood. Brave man.

When the house lights dim, I wait for Alexa's cue to pull the curtain while Drew finds his place center stage. I like being backstage. All of the audience's attention is focused on the actors while we stay quiet in the dark. From a small folding chair, I listen for my three cues, watching actors change costumes for their next entrance. They switch in and out of their characters in the blink of their exits, focused. I could *never* get out there, exposed to those waiting eyes.

At the end, the applause is everywhere at once. Because it's closing night, Sara, her arms full of roses, pulls me out onstage to bow. The lights sting my eyes; the faces of the audience float and shift.

Somehow through the glare and floating faces, I know that Sam sees me see him standing in the back. He's ignored me for two weeks, avoided my eyes in class. Still, I can't help but smile a little. He gives me a short, quick wave, a salute in midair. The house lights come up. I blink into the softer glow, looking again for Sam, but he's pushing through the heavy doors into the late fall night.

CHAPTER 10
HUMAN NATURE

...I turn twelve on New Year's Eve, and for some reason I can't totally explain, my mother decides to throw me a Madonna party, maybe because she had a Madonna party on her twelfth birthday. People in all versions of Madonna's rock-star evolution crowd into the living room and bump and grind and...vogue. I sit under the dining-room table and eat an entire package of Nutter Butters...

"YOU **NEED TO GET TO** class, please." The yard lady whose name nobody knows stands on the concrete pavement several yards away. "Now. Read your love letters in class."

This last comment is unnecessary and a little rude. Still, I gather up my backpack, refold my note, and silently obey orders. I am not one to talk back or make quippy remarks when there could be detention at the other end of it. I can feel her watch me walk the quiet path toward the math building, her walkie-talkie whispering at her hip.

The note reads:

Hey, my friend: If you're going to waste your time here, at least waste it with me. Listen to Green Day's "Sassafras Roots."

I found it wedged into the plastic sleeve of my binder at the end of lunch. Unsigned and written in quick, black letters. I know that song. I love that song.

I want the note to be from Sam. Maybe more than I actually think it is from him, I want it to be. That would be cool—a cryptic apology of sorts. But inside me, stalking my optimism, is reality. The images of him with Amber, she leaning in close enough that her hair drapes his shoulder; Cass clutching his sleeve; his heroic run of the football; his brisk exit from the theater.

Chances are, he didn't write this note. Did he? Does he know I keep songs in my journal? Write down lyrics to cement the memories in ink across the page?

In math, I rub the folded edge of the note between my fingers until the blue lines of the binder paper are gone, and the paper is as soft as Kleenex. I try to concentrate on the lesson going on at the board, solving for x, finding the value for y. The value of y. Why. Why did he kiss me? Why did he kiss me and then ignore me for weeks?

I look at my binder. My notes are a mess, and finally I just give up, hoping that the textbook explains the concept well enough for me to figure it out on my own. I want to read the note again, looking for the words beneath the words. A clue. The subtext,

Alexa would call it. In theater, the actors have to figure out what's going on under the lines in order to play the character truthfully. Ms. Hecca does a lot of subtext games with them at rehearsal. To get at the honesty of the line, she says. What is the subtext here in my little secret binder note?

I tuck the note away in my sweatshirt pocket, letting it sleep alongside my Walkman. I don't want to risk it getting taken away.

• • •

I decide that I've been imagining things.

Watching Sam laughing with his friends in the quad at lunch, drinking a soda, thumping Justin Wallen on the shoulder, I realize that maybe he hasn't been avoiding me at all. I mean, I haven't exactly approached him.

This is ridiculous. I should just talk to him. Determined, I cross the lawn to the stone picnic table he sits on with his friends. Small clumps of lunching students brave the chilly wind. The hum of their conversations tickles my ears, or maybe that's the wind, but I feel detached from all of them. A boat suddenly unanchored from a steady dock. Adrift, I slow my stride as I near him, aware that the boys at the table have stopped talking and are watching my approach. Zach Wilcox follows the gaze I have fixed on Sam, his eyebrows curious.

"Hi, Sam," I say when I'm close enough to have to say something.

He averts his eyes. "Um, hey." He takes a quick drink of his soda and shrugs at Zach.

I know the blood has gone to my face. It has to go somewhere, as I'm certain it's no longer in my feet or my hands or my legs. No matter, with bloodless limbs, I turn away, but not before I hear them ask him, "Who's that?"

And hear him respond, "I don't know. A girl from English."

I head straight for the bathroom, hearing and seeing nothing, and push my way into a stall. I close the door behind me, latching the silver arm that flips up and over to lock the stall, and stare at the back of the door. Scrawls of black-marker proclamations, both personal and general: *Jim Trainer is a hottie…Erica Greenich is a bitch…this school sucks ass!*

I lie and tell myself I won't cry. Maybe he kissed me on a dare? Kiss the new girl. Funny football locker room joke.

My eyes are drawn to the side of the stall where someone has covered half the wall with fist-sized black-ink words. A poem. And not your usual bathroom insult or proclamation. My eyes wash over it.

Then I read it again.

Read me, read me here alone, walled off
In a room to hide in this place of unending
Night. This shadow place. You race to find
What's right here in front of your two-
Faced space. Read it. And open your eyes.
All of the lies, the screaming, dreaming lack
Of focus pleading with the only one who sees
The truth. Not you. Not me too. This night's
Too dark, split apart, to have dreams.

The words hit me. I'm sitting in the night of this poem. In my life, I've been a traveler too many times, a visitor in other people's hometowns. Each time I've set a suitcase down, my other hand has been ready to pick it up again. I'm packed before I even unpack. Until here. I see Sam again, shrugging me away, sipping his soda. He swatted me like a fly.

This is the worst moment of my life. I had the beach, his smile in the late afternoon sun, his kiss tasting of air and salt, and now I'm sitting in this crappy bathroom stall staring at graffiti on a door. I look at the last line again: "*This night's too dark, split apart, to have dreams.*"

CHAPTER 11
HARD TO EXPLAIN

From the shadow of the tire swing in the front yard, I watch my mother and a nameless man drink wine on the front porch of the small duplex in Gilroy, the air thick with the smell of garlic fields. In the summer night, strains of Cowboy Junkies filter from the upstairs radio, washing the dark with their steady, hypnotic melody, and I feel like I could just swing here, back and forth, forever...

I SEE HIM TALKING TO his dad in the bakery and almost duck back into the cake-mix aisle to avoid him. I haven't showered since Friday morning, and I've been wearing the same jeans for three days. I just want to go home, re-cocoon myself into the blanket I've been hibernating in all weekend on the living-room couch, and let Mom make me brownies because she says brownies will make me feel better.

I hesitate, and it is in this tiny pocket of time that he sees me.

"Hey, Calle," he says, biting his lip and glancing at his dad.

"Hi." I wave awkwardly, a cereal box under my arm. Mom forgot to buy Golden Grahams again. I walk closer, wishing I could smooth my hair down without looking like I was trying to fix it. His father, who shares Sam's broad shoulders, is rounder than Sam in the face, and his curly hair has turned a white gray, like cotton balls stuck to his skull. Sam must look more like his mom.

"What's up?" Sam doesn't introduce me.

"Nothing. Brownies." I hold up the box like a visual aid, and it takes me a minute to realize I'm not holding brownies. I'm holding cereal. Heat rises in my face. What an idiot. I should walk away, but I don't.

He doesn't seem to notice, just studies the floor.

"Okay, Sam." His father's voice is deep but rings of Sam's. "I'm going to be in the office. Okay?"

"Sure, Dad."

"You need to call if that happens again. You don't have to try to handle it on your own."

Sam narrows his eyes a bit but nods. "I know."

"Nice to meet you," he says to the space over my head and then disappears down the next aisle.

"Thing is, we didn't actually meet," I say, studying Sam's interest in the floor, willing him to make eye contact with me. He doesn't. I try to keep a scowl off my face.

"Calle…" he starts and then rethinks it.

Somewhere before the pause becomes a chasm, I decide to push ahead. "So what's going on with you?"

"Nothing."

I feel stupid holding the cereal box, and we are in the middle of a grocery store where about half the town is wandering the aisles. Still, I don't know if I'll have another chance to ask him. "Why did you blow me off on Friday?"

"What?" He pretends to look confused. The attempt would be almost comical if I didn't feel like throwing my Golden Grahams at him.

I raise my eyebrows. I've seen my mother do this, a look that says, "Are you kidding me with this crap?" I'm hoping for the look now.

He falls for it. "Look, I didn't mean anything by it, okay? It's not a big deal."

"It was a big deal to me." I don't tell him how embarrassing it actually was.

He sighs and looks down the aisle, looks behind him, looks everywhere but at me. "Calle, this isn't really a good time."

"When is a good time?"

He runs his fingers through his smoothed hair, sending it in all directions. His lips pinch together. Finally, he looks at me directly. "I can't talk about it."

"Did I do something wrong?"

"No. It has nothing to do with you."

"You ignoring me has nothing to do with me?" I don't like how loud this comes out, and I bite the next sentence off before it escapes me.

He darts a look around. "Will you lower your voice?"

"Sorry." I am sorry. I don't want to make a scene.

He's flustered; I see red creeping across his cheeks. "Look, don't be pissed. It's not you. I have a lot going on."

I hear him walk away down the aisle behind me. I don't feel like Golden Grahams or brownies anymore. The cool grocery-store air suffocates me, so I abandon the box on the end display of canned corn and tuna fish and find the nearest exit.

. . .

"Calle, wait." For the briefest of moments I think it's Sam calling me, and the surge in my chest turns me around. Then I see Drew, with Alexa close behind him, hurrying out of the sliding doors of the market. His blue cape flutters behind him, making him look like an out-of-shape superhero. I stop to wait for them. Deflated.

"Jeez," Drew says, breathing and clutching his chest. "I wasn't expecting a cardiovascular workout today." I start to smile at his "Spear Brittany" T-shirt and then realize they must have seen my little exchange with Sam. Why else would Drew run?

"Hey," Alexa says, her eyes worried. "Umm, we just saw you with Sam Atkins. In there." She motions to the store. "We saw you guys, umm, talking." Drew raises his eyebrows at this understatement.

We stand on the tiny path by the main road while cars whoosh past us, kicking up tiny whirls of litter and dust. I focus on the passing cars and wait for the inevitable.

Alexa tucks a lock of hair behind her ear. In the early winter light, her hair is the thick red of new brick. "Are you two…" she hesitates. "Are you two involved?"

I shrug, aware that this is an admission. I do not miss the look they exchange.

"Cal," Drew says, "He's not really the best idea."

"He's not an idea. He's a person."

Alexa clears her throat and speaks slowly, like I'm a child. "He's got a lot of problems. With his mom."

My breath catches. In all my guessing and wondering, I never for a moment thought that Drew or Alexa or any of them would know anything. That they would be able to explain it to me. I'm so stupid. They've lived here their whole lives. "What do you two know?"

"They're really secretive about it," Drew says. "His dad especially. There are a lot of rumors. Alcohol's the one I've heard the most. That she gets sent away for it."

"Sent away?"

Alexa nods. "No one really knows what happened with her. Sam's always been really walled off about it. I think that's why he hangs with the group he hangs with. He doesn't have to talk about it. He can just play football and go to parties and…" she considers, genuinely puzzled, "and whatever else they do."

This doesn't answer anything for me. "Then why'd he kiss me?"

"He kissed you?" Drew doesn't hide his surprise.

"Is that hard to believe?"

Alexa sighs, looking slightly uncomfortable. "Yes."

The word is a slap. "Well, he did."

Alexa explains, "Calle, it just doesn't make sense. Sam Atkins doesn't veer from his group. Why would he? He's got so much going on at home. Why would he make his life hard at school?"

"Why would I make his life hard? Am I some sort of freak?"

"You're not a freak," Alexa says. "You're just not..." She seems to have run out of words, but there's no need for her to finish. I get it. It's always been this way.

CHAPTER 12
FATHER OF MINE

...Mom hid my Everclear CD for three days—threatening its destruction if I insist on listening to it repeatedly—but I find it wedged in behind the Costco-sized mac-and-cheese boxes while she's at work. I lie face down on my bed and play it over and over until she wrenches it from my CD player and breaks it into a thousand pieces, telling me to find a new favorite band...fast...

MY MOTHER'S DRAWERS ARE A tangled mess of bras and tank tops, leggings and balled-up pairs of jeans. How can someone who always looks so put together start every morning with this? A tiny nudge of guilt quiets the critic in me; I am, after all, rifling through her drawers without permission.

I know she has a windbreaker in here somewhere, a red one, that folds itself into a pouch, but she's not around to ask. An hour ago, standing outside Bay View Foods, Alexa and Drew insisted I come with them to the beach for an impromptu early-winter picnic.

They're planning to meet some other drama kids there. Maybe the wind and sand will erase my run-in with Sam.

Catching sight of the slippery red nylon pouch, I pull it free of a pair of black stockings. I almost close the drawer when my eyes catch on a corner of creamy paper poking through the neck hole of one of Mom's workout shirts. I pluck it out, and the corner becomes the full body of an envelope. An envelope with my name written in careful black ink on the front. An envelope I've never seen.

The return address is from Jake Winter. Winter? My heart quickens. I pause long enough to listen for any sign of my mother returning, and the silence of the house prods me forward. The envelope has been carefully opened. My reopening it will leave no trace.

Inside is a letter from my father.

Calle,

My guess is that you probably won't even get to read this letter. Your mother has become quite skilled at intercepting anything I try to send you, any phone calls I try to make. But if you do read this, I want you to know that I'm sorry I haven't been in your life...

I look quickly to the date at the top of the letter. Three years my mother has kept this letter tucked in the chaos of her clothing, moving it from place to place with us. Hidden.

I have never gotten over finding your crib empty that morning your mother took you away. I still remember the sound of the rain against the windows of your empty room.

What? I reread the last lines again and again. "…your mother took you away." But he left us. When I was a baby. Walked out on us. Didn't he? I race through the remainder of the letter. He's been trying to find me, keeps missing us in our moves, wants to see me, know me. He leaves an email address, and the letter is signed, "Your father, Jake Winter."

My father's name is Jake Winter. Not Smith like my last name. I think of the picture tucked in my journal, not taken in winter but of Jake *Winter*. My mind capsizes with questions. Why am I Smith? Why has my mom told me my whole life that he left us for his music? Why hasn't she let me meet him? The letter is an open heart beating in my lap.

● ● ●

My mother lied to me.

The structure of a lie—of something purposefully told or with-held—is strange to me. My mother doesn't lie. At least I thought she didn't. I have never had the type of relationships that require lies, even small ones. This year, though, the lies I have been dodging all my life have caught up to me. My fair share all at once. Sam. Now my mother. And I have this father sitting out in the world somewhere without an answer to his letter, wondering about me. About his daughter.

I didn't go to the picnic yesterday, and Alexa seemed hurt when she left me sitting here on the aluminum bench by the theater minutes ago. I could've told her; she would've understood. But this is mine. The letter in my hands is a thin paper, like onion skin, with thick greasy letters that march in order across the page. I look again at the bottom: "Your father, Jake," it says, the signature now a familiar secret. Jake. Jake Winter.

Sitting here, I am full of the metal-colored sky. All around me, blue December air coats the world with a strange, cool light. I watch the students flood the exits of the school. They seem robotic in the blue light, magnified. The light brings out the clothes of students wearing color, but the ones in gray, in black, in earth tones are muted like they've been washed too many times. My own sweat-shirt is the blue of the light, and I imagine I am camouflaged in it.

Last night, my mother looked at me only slightly funny when I coughed twice and told her I was fighting something and going to bed early. I should confront her. Demand an answer. My father's email address is tucked in my pocket. I should walk down to the media center and write to him. Confront Mom or write Dad. Instead, I sit on this metal bench and stare at the sky.

• • •

Mom's sulky lately, wearing the same sweatshirt days in a row. Like me, but not like her. I haven't seen Rob much; he drifts in after a run or work or the gym but usually not until much past eight or nine. I hear their heated whispers late at night when they think I'm sleeping. They aren't newlyweds anymore.

I don't want to think about my mother. Or Rob. The computer in front of me has given me more important things to worry about. Before school this morning, I wrote my father. Just a short "Here's my email; here's where I'm living" note. Painfully short. After school, I checked to see if he'd written back. I hadn't expected a response, but I also hadn't expected this. My letter sits returned in its slender slot of the inbox. Rejected. His address no longer exists.

"Hey, stranger." Alexa pulls a chair up to the computer.

I quickly delete the rejected letter and close my email.

"Who're you writing to?"

"Just a friend in San Diego." I sign off, fumbling a smile. Alexa knows me better but also knows not to push.

"Hey," she begins again. "I'm sorry if I was a witch to you yesterday about the picnic."

"No big deal." I shrug. While I really don't think it's a big deal, I know I appear aloof and strange.

She darts a look around the library, which is now inhabited only by a few diehards and the pale light of late afternoon. She lowers her voice anyway. "Look. It's none of my business and none of Drew's business who you like or who you want to spend time with. We were just trying to give you some advice is all, because we don't want you to get hurt."

I nod. This time, I manage to pull off a reasonably believable smile. "Seriously, Lex. It's no problem. I have a lot on my mind. A lot that has nothing to do with Sam or school or anything here."

She nods knowingly. "Parents."

"Yeah."

"I get that."

I pull my backpack onto my lap and wait for her to say more. Any second, I'm bound to spill the letter to Alexa, and I really don't want to do that.

Then her face lights. She grabs me around the wrist. "You know what we should do?"

"What?"

"We'll go to Tala's and have her read fortune cookies for you."

"Have her do what?"

"Read fortune cookies." I must look completely befuddled because she releases my wrist, laughing, and says, "I know it sounds nuts, but Tala's really into this, and it's a lot of fun to watch her."

. . .

Tala has the bedroom of someone who's lived there her whole life. The walls are papered with her past, layers of all her years: posters of ballerinas, Hello Kitty, Colbie Caillat; concert stubs and a Cal Bears pennant; a princess crown; hundreds of pictures of Toby.

Alexa and I sit on the floor in the center of a giant purple throw rug shot with silver glitter strands.

"Wow," I say, my eyes straying over the pictures of Tala and Toby—at Disneyland, at the beach, at a birthday party. "She has a lot of pictures of Toby."

Alexa makes a face. "Those two are practically married."

Tala pushes open the door, carrying a tray of sodas and a clear sack of fortune cookies. "Okay, folks," she says. "Fortune time." After setting the tray on the bed, she drapes a sheer red cloth over the lampshade, bathing the room in rose-colored light.

"Where did you get all of those cookies?" I ask. There must be a hundred cookies in the bag.

"Eli's parents own Mandarin Garden."

"They do?"

Alexa nods. "His mom's from China; that's where he gets that hair." I love Eli's shock of glossy, black hair. Lately, he's let it grow long, razored just above his dark eyes.

"Pick six cookies," Tala tells me, opening the top of the sack and holding it out.

I select six cookies and hand them back to her. She takes a white cloth napkin from the tray, carefully spreading it out on the purple rug. One by one, she lays the cookies in a neat, even row. She closes her eyes; the lids are thick with taupe shadow. I dart a look at Alexa, who smiles, covering her mouth to stifle a giggle.

"Alexa," Tala says, her eyes still closed.

"Sorry, Tal." Alexa fixes her face to serious.

Tala opens her eyes. Carefully, she cracks each cookie in one hand, crumbling it like sand through her fingers, and smooths each white slip of fortune onto the purple rug until all six slips sit in a perforated line, their inks varying colors of the rainbow.

"Now, I'll tell you your fortune," she says seriously, eyes half-lidded in concentration. I watch her closely, taking in the elfin lines of her face, the narrow angled jaw, the almond eyes. With the sides of her blond hair braided into a knot at the back of her head, she looks straight out of *The Lord of the Rings*.

"Okay," she says, her fingertips grazing the fortunes. "The first slip is for family. It says 'you will be strong in the face of trouble.'" Her voice is whispery, and I feel ridiculous. Still, I try to look intently at her as she squints at the fortune. "Your strength is what's key here. Emotionally. Not physically. You'll need to be strong."

Something hits at the pit of me, a clawing at my middle. In the silly rose light of the room, on the silver-threaded purple rug, I know this means my mom. And my dad. Will I ever find him? I lean in closer.

"The second slip says 'you see the world for what it is.' This slip is for friendship. Red ink. Look for it in unexpected places." Tala sighs, tucking a stray lock of hair behind her ears. "Friends will come from different sides of your life but they are all valid—except for one." Alexa frowns slightly; I try to ignore it.

"The third slip is for personal self. It says 'you give of yourself.' But you need to take care of yourself first, before you take care of someone else." She stops, studying the slip closely, and then looks the same way at me. "This is especially important."

"Okay," I whisper. Alexa's eyebrows raise and she averts her eyes, studying the now shadowy pictures on the walls.

"The fourth slip is for dreams. It says 'there is safety in your loved ones.' This one's conflicted," she says, her eyebrows in a quizzical tilt on her brow. "You want safety, but you want love. And love for you isn't safe." I shift uncomfortably on the floor, my feet tingling. "You might have to choose."

"What do you mean?" I take a sip of my Sprite, my stomach turning.

Tala looks at me. "Safety or love. Let's see…" She runs her finger over the fifth slip. "Your fifth slip is for love. It says 'the road of life is long.' It's not a clear road. You have options for both."

"Options?"

"If you protect yourself, you'll choose safety. If you choose love, you don't protect yourself. We'll have to see what the sixth slip reads."

"What's the sixth slip for?"

"Fate." Alexa leans in a little, watching Tala's face closely. "This is the one that ties the others together, that controls them."

"What does it say?" I find myself caring, hoping for some sign, as stupid as all of this is.

"The ink is blue, which means water will play a key part. It says 'the universe provides happiness to those who want it.'" I think of the wide arms of ocean that stretch out nearby. "The universe wants you to be happy because you want other people to be happy."

"So my fate is to be happy?" I sit back. How generic.

"If you want it to be." Her shrug is a dismissal. She begins to pick up each slip, placing them in a purple ceramic bowl. She drops a lit match into the glossy belly of the bowl, and the tiny white slips curl in flames and fade to ash.

• • •

My mother is washing vegetables in the sink and doesn't hear me come in. I watch the sharp lines of her back from the doorway as she scrubs at a yellow squash. She had her hair highlighted last week, and it falls past her shoulders in glossy, varied strips.

"I found the letter."

She jumps, water splashing. "Jeez, Calle." She doesn't turn around but leans instead on the edge of the sink.

"Sorry."

She begins to mop the counter with a dish towel. "What are you talking about? What letter?"

"The one from my father."

At this, she turns, her hands tangled in the dish towel. "You went through my drawers?"

"You weren't here, and I needed a windbreaker." She will try to make this my fault; I know it. "Don't change the subject."

Her face flushes. "I think the subject has to do with you going through my personal property."

"The letter was my personal property; it was addressed to me."

She tosses the dish towel on the counter. For a moment, something strange crosses her face, a ghost of fear moving across her anger. "You weren't old enough to see that letter when it came." Opening a cabinet, she pulls a cutting board down and begins to line up the vegetables on it.

"When would I be old enough?"

She begins chopping a carrot into Life-Saver-sized circles and doesn't answer.

"Mom? When were you planning on showing me the letter?"

She starts on a zucchini. "I don't have to explain myself to you. I'm your mother. I had my reasons."

"What were they?" I take a breath, knowing that if I start to shout, she'll start to shout. "Don't pull the 'because I'm your mother' argument because you know it's crap."

The knife pauses above the yellow squash she's cutting into disks. "Calle. Your father left when you were eight months old. He has no right to contact you. He's a father in biological terms only. Don't imagine it's something else."

"He says you left him."

"Well, that's obviously ridiculous. He left to be with his band. I've told you a thousand times." Chop, chop, chop. I think she might take her finger off.

"Why would he say you left?"

She slams the knife down. "Why does Jake do anything?"

Tears threaten my lashes, and I swipe at them. "I don't know, Mom," I say to her back. "I don't know him. You haven't let me know him. I didn't even know his real last name!"

She picks up the knife again and doesn't respond. The vegetable discs turn to half circles, to wedges, and finally to bits.

"Have there been other times?" I ask.

She dips her head, intent on her chopping. "What?"

I hold up the letter. "Is this it? Is this the only one?"

She whirls on me, the knife skittering across the counter. "What are you saying, Calle?"

"I want to know why you've been hiding him from me!"

"So now suddenly you want your father in your life? Is that it?" She yanks open a cupboard and pulls out a wok.

"I want the choice."

Retrieving the knife, she uses it to slide all of the vegetables into the wok. "No."

"No?"

She sets the cutting board and the knife carefully into the sink, turns to me, and repeats, "No." I open my mouth, but she cuts me off, her voice low and certain. "Listen to me, Calle. That man... those things in the letter aren't true. He's...his reality is different than what really happened."

She pauses, appraises me. I can see tears forming in her eyes, her struggle to keep them at bay. "Calle, there are things about your father, things you don't know..." she trails off. Finally, she whispers, "I made the mistake of bringing him into my life. I will not bring him into yours. You are *not* to have contact with him."

My chest tightens but threatens to burst; I want to run, but am cemented to the cracked, tan linoleum beneath me. "You can't do that," I try to say, but I am not sure it comes out. Collecting myself—like tumbled laundry, piece by piece—I manage to hoist my backpack onto my shoulder and step backward from the room.

"Calle…" my mother starts.

"Don't," I say, still walking backward, gaining momentum. "You made mistakes, but your mistakes aren't mine. He might not have wanted you—that doesn't mean he doesn't want me."

She doesn't try to stop me from leaving.

CHAPTER 13
SMALL WORLD

...Mom humming an Ani DiFranco song in the slash light of the neon diner sign, eating a garden salad with ranch dressing, and picking at my fries she promised she wouldn't eat. We sit at outside plastic tables. The highway shifts and ripples in the heat of the evening sunset as the waitress brings us iced teas on the house. She and my mom chat a bit. Turns out, Mom knows the waitress at this tiny road-stop along the I-5. We've been here before it seems...

THE SUN SET ONLY MINUTES ago, leaving a bruised sky. The head-lights of an oncoming truck cut into the paste-gray light left over. The truck slows to a stop next to me. My heart beats a warning. As nomadic as I've been all of my life, strangers still make me nervous.

"What the hell are you doing?" Cass is small behind the wheel of the truck. "Get in." That I'm too cold to argue squashes any initial curiosity about what she's doing driving since she's a freshman too. I pull open the door and climb in next to her on the bench seat.

The truck is very old (not a Ford), and smells of motor oil and pipe smoke. The vinyl seats are cracked and patched with peeling duct tape. A jagged, horizontal slash bisects the window. As I warm up, I can't help but take note that this slash is right in her sight line.

"What're you doing?"

"Just walking."

She continues on down the road, one hand draped loosely over the wheel, the other fiddling with the tuner on the portable stereo next to her on the seat. She hits on Theory of a Deadman's "Not Meant to Be" and turns up the volume.

She puts both hands on the wheel. "I love this song." She sings loudly over the music.

I settle back in the seat as she curves around toward the downtown. Lights begin to click on, the downtown becoming a spattering of lit windows and bright signs. Cass hurls the truck around a corner, and we pull into the drive-thru of Burger Mania. She bumps to a stop at the order station, which is shaped like a giant cheeseburger.

"You want fries?"

"I don't have any money."

"No sweat." To the order station she says, "Harper? You working?"

The plastic cheeseburger comes to life, a crackling voice emerging. "Hey, Cass."

"Two orders of fries and two Cokes." She looks at me. "Coke?"

I nod.

She repeats, "Yeah, two Cokes."

"Okeydokey," says the crackle voice. She jerks the car ahead.

A man leans at the window. He is well into his sixties, barrel bellied, and pocked with tattoos. His blue eyes are so pale they almost match the whites of his eyes. "Who's your friend?"

Cass leans on her window, hooking a thumb at me. "This is Calle."

"Pleasure," says Harper.

"Nice to meet you," I say.

He disappears into Burger Mania and then returns with a sack of food and two Cokes in white Styrofoam cups. "Fries and extra ketchup. I threw some burgers in there, kid. You need to eat."

Cass smiles at him. With him, she is without all of the knocked-about attitude that she drags to school every day. "You're the best, Harp."

He winks. Another car pulls in behind us. "Say hi to your uncle for me."

"Will do," Cass says and negotiates the truck back onto the street.

My mouth waters with the smell of the food in the truck.

"Want to go to the beach?" She digs her hand into the bag and extracts a few fries. Chewing, she says, "We can hang in the parking lot at Clover."

"That sounds good." I ache to follow her lead on the fries. I'm starving, but I wait for her to offer. She doesn't.

At the beach, she turns off the engine and the radio. She cracks open a window. The sound of the ocean pours in around us. Cass rifles through the bag and pulls out the food. Flattening the bag, she squeezes ketchup into a mound and drags a fry through it.

Finally I reach over and pick up a burger. I unwrap the yellow paper. Since Mom went vegetarian, I haven't eaten anything but veggie burgers, and the first bite of the real thing rushes through my body.

"Yum," I say, dipping fries into the ketchup. "Thanks."

Cass pulls from her Coke. "Sure." She studies me. I slow down a bit on the burger, certain I must look like a starved child, and use a paper napkin to wipe my face. Cass unwraps her burger, opens it, and picks off the flimsy pickles. She squeezes two more ketchup packets onto the meat and then pats the top. Eating, she watches the moonlight on the waves. She takes small, delicate bites. "So, just walking, huh?"

Swallowing, I say, "My mom and I had a fight."

"What about?"

"My father."

"Is he being a jerk?"

I shrug, wadding the burger wrapper into a ball.

"I don't know him at all." I tell her my story.

She looks at me, her eyes shadowed. "I don't have a dad either."

We both watch the waves, not totally sure what to say now.

"I'm sorry," I finally whisper.

She shrugs. "What happened with your mom?"

After telling her about the letter, I say, "She didn't think I should see it, doesn't think he should be in my life."

She rattles the ice in her Coke as she drinks it. "What do you think?"

I look at the sand, colorless in the glow of the bare moon. "I don't know. Sometimes I wonder what he's like. If he's…"

"Like you?" she finishes for me.

"I guess, yeah. Or if I'm like him."

"That's normal." She finishes her fries and starts to roll all the trash into the flattened bag, keeping the ketchup in the middle.

With the sound of the ocean keeping out the silence, a sudden bravery comes over me. I change the subject. "What's the deal with Sam?"

"What about him?" Her whole tone has changed.

The edge of it erodes any bravery. "Umm," I stumble, "I just wondered about his mom."

She eyes me carefully. "What have you heard?"

"Nothing really. Alcohol. That kind of stuff."

"She's not an alcoholic, if that's what you've heard from that crazy Alexa."

She starts the truck and backs out of the parking lot in one clean motion. In less than a minute, we're back on the street heading toward my house.

"Alexa's not crazy."

"She has a big mouth."

I don't answer, caught between wanting to defend Alexa and knowing that Alexa does, in fact, tend to have a lot of opinions about people—and no fears about sharing them.

I say, "She's been really nice to me."

"Whatever." Cass turns up the volume on the radio, our words replaced with a pounding Kings of Leon song.

When she drops me in front of my house, she says, "Don't believe everything you hear."

CHAPTER 14

COMPLICATED

...with a flourish, Mom sets the steaming pizza in the middle of the brown Formica table and brushes a lock of hair from her eyes with the back of her hand. She absentmindedly taps her foot to the Avril Lavigne blaring from corner speakers. Her new waitressing job is at Joe's, a pizza parlor that consists of a jukebox, twelve rickety tables, and caramelized lighting that fails to hide the holes in the carpet. The place is a dump, but the pepperoni pizza is cheesy and greasy and wonderful...

NOT SICK, i PLAY HOOKY for the first time in my life. The empty house a silent animal curled around me, I sprawl on my bed listening to Bob Dylan, Sara Bareilles, Arcade Fire. I listen to Springsteen's *Nebraska* album all the way through, even though my mom says my generation doesn't have the attention span to listen to an album start to finish. But I listen. And cry. And listen. And cry. At a particularly dark point of the mid-morning, when the sky outside is a clenched fist of gray clouds, I raid my mother's room again, listening to *The Wall*, the Pink Floyd CD she only listens to when men leave her.

In this dark moment, I find the drawer.

It is a small, thin drawer at the base of my mom's dresser. I pull at it. Locked. I search through her side table for the key, and check the pockets of her coats and the hollows of her shoes. No key. I almost give up when I spy the brown stuffed bear she's always had. One black button eye is missing; the fur is matted with age; and it wears a tie-dyed shirt with black writing that reads, "Jerry lives."

I pull it from the shelf and squeeze. Something hard bites into my palm, and I notice that the seam of one of the bear's arms has been pulled loose. Victorious, I wiggle my finger around inside and come up with a small, metal key.

Inside, the drawer is shallow and lined with midnight felt. I find a pile of snapshots, mostly Mom with random guys. Some I remember. Some I don't. There is a baby picture of me, my face bunched into a scowl. I smile at another picture of me at four or five with a Tom Petty shirt that grazes the top of my tiny feet. The back of the picture says, "Calle—my wildflower—age five."

Under the pictures, I find a black folder, frayed and graying at the edges. I open it and flip through pages of Mom's handwritten notes: strange addresses, cities, and phone numbers of people whose names I don't recognize. Folded in half is a newspaper clipping of my dad, younger than the other picture, hair longer, in front of a drum set, the name Wonderland scrawled across it. His band. I'm careful not to let tears drip on the clipping.

In the corner of the drawer, near the back, I find another newspaper piece, just a small slim square with a list of names. One name stands out:

JAKE WINTER, CONVICTED, AGGRAVATED ASSAULT.

My stomach feels full of push-pins. He was in jail, my father. Maybe he still is. I tuck the slip of newspaper back into the drawer, guilt flooding me. I make sure everything is back in place and then close the drawer. I wriggle the key back into the bear and shut the door to my mom's room.

I turn up the stereo, sit on the couch with a bag of Doritos I smuggled in past my mom, and contemplate my father, the criminal. I invent scenes in my head that would explain his conviction, *aggravated assault*. Maybe he assaulted a landlord or a stranger in a bar, one of his bandmates…one of my mom's lovers?

When the doorbell rings at three-thirty, I am in the midst of playing The Who's "Baba O'Riley" for the fourth time in a row, shouting the lyrics at the top of my lungs. Embarrassed, I venture to the door in my pajamas, blue ones with tiny puffs of clouds. Through the peephole I discover Eli, his hands full of book bags and brown sacks.

I open the door. "Hi."

His razored hair slices angles over his eyes, and he shakes his head to clear his vision. "Hey." He holds up the bags. "You're rocking out in here, huh?"

I shrug. "Just listening to some music." I hurry to turn it off and notice I have Doritos cheese under my nails.

He waits in the hall. When I return, he says, "I brought the homework you missed. And some food." Smiling, he looks at me. "Nice pj's."

"Oh. Thanks."

In the entryway, he dumps the book bags. He looks around, squinting in the dim light of the house—we don't have many windows. "Kitchen?" he asks.

I point through the doorway to the kitchen and then follow him in. He searches the cabinets for bowls, some spoons, two glasses. "I brought chicken soup and orange juice," he says, smiling over his shoulder at me. I smile back mostly at his bright yellow, long-sleeved shirt the color and texture of a rain slicker. And at the soup and orange juice.

He pours the soup from a large Styrofoam container, using a fork to push noodles into the bowls. The smell fills the room, and my stomach stands alert, having consumed only half the bag of Doritos today. "Thanks," I say.

"Everyone needs chicken soup when they're sick, especially chicken soup from Greta's Diner—it's the best."

He sets the bowls on the breakfast bar, and I slide onto a stool in front of one. He sits next to me. Through slurping spoonfuls, he asks, "So. You have a cold?"

"I just sort of feel under the weather."

He nods. "There's something going around."

Is there ever. It's called Lying Mother-itis.

We finish our soup, and I clear the bowls into the sink.

"I had Drew get your English homework, and Tala got your math assignment; it's just a worksheet. She said it takes five minutes."

I run water over the bowls and put them in the dishwasher. "Thanks, Eli. You didn't have to do this."

"I don't mind."

"It's really nice."

"I'm a nice guy."

"Very true." I run a sponge unnecessarily over the counters, aware that Eli is watching me closely. The intensity of his gaze makes me run the sponge back over the clean counter.

He says, "I wrote the note."

At first, I can think only of my father's letter, of the slim line of text marking him a criminal. Then I understand: Eli's my secret binder-note poet.

I have no idea what to say to him, to those dark, steady eyes.

He clears his throat. "You hadn't said anything, so I figured I needed to be a little less cryptic."

I look at him, my stomach swimming. "I wasn't sure it was you."

"Who else would it be?" His voice hints that there is more behind this question.

I shrug, thankful for the counter between us. "I don't know."

"Sam Atkins?"

"No," I answer too quickly.

Eli's jaw twitches. "You know the guy's a real jerk?"

I flare. "He's not."

Eli picks up his half-empty orange juice glass but sets it down again just as quickly. "In seventh grade," he starts, and then takes a quick drink after all. "In seventh grade, he put me through hell because I'm half-Chinese. Made fun of my eyes. He's a total jock prick, Calle."

I can't believe that about Sam, not if he's been through so much stuff with his mom. But "I'm sorry," is all I can manage. I have never seen Eli so serious, no jokes.

He shakes his soft curtain of hair. "Forget it." Standing abruptly, he hits his head on the overhang of the cupboard. "Ouch, dammit!"

I hurry around the counter. "Are you okay?"

He smiles, embarrassed. "Sure. Probably knocked some sense into me."

A large red welt is appearing behind the hair. He rubs at it gingerly. "Do you want some ice?"

As he shakes his head, I reach out and touch his forehead, just barely graze my fingers along the bruise, but as I do so, he leans in and kisses me. For a second, I let him. His lips are soft, and he tastes salty and citrusy, but as quickly as I'd accepted his kiss, I pull away from it.

He doesn't say anything. Doesn't apologize or try to explain it—just looks at me closely, then steps by me toward the entryway. Not turning, I can hear him pick up his backpack and close the door softly behind him.

I sit at the counter and bury my head in my arms. I should have gone to school.

• • •

Drew sees them before I do.

Under the eave of the library, hidden only accidentally by shadow, stand Sam and Amber. Actually, Sam stands. Amber sort of leans into him, all of her weight cemented into his, so that if he took a sudden step back, she would go toppling onto the ground. I would love to see that—her spilling head first into the pavement.

But instead, I watch him kiss her. If they are going to topple over, they'll go over together. Even by high-school standards, their display is revolting.

Drew agrees. "Get a room." His voice, though, is anxious, and I know he's studying my face.

"Yeah," I manage, attempting to mask my emotions, which is hard because I don't even know what I'm feeling—anger, jealousy, disbelief. I probably look like I'm going to puke.

"Let's get out of here," Drew says, vaguely pulling on the elbow of my sweatshirt. He sounds embarrassed, and I realize that I am literally gaping at them. People are following my gaze and starting to whisper. "Come on, Calle, let's go."

I will my legs to follow him, one after the other, until we've rounded a corner and my heart stops pounding in my chest. "We should get your fries," I say, staring blankly at the ground. Fries, after all, had been our whole reason for walking through the quad. "Class starts soon." I realize that I can't even remember what class I have. Biology? Do I go to biology class first period?

"They've been on and off since seventh grade." I notice the soft edge in Drew's voice. "But it's really more her than him. I give that chick kudos for perseverance."

"He didn't look too unhappy," I say, still studying the ground.

"A guy only has so much willpower, Calle. She throws herself at him. You can't blame him."

At this, I look at him. "Can't I?"

Drew flushes. "I just mean…Look, he isn't the type of guy to tell her no."

"Well, that's just great. It is." The unfairness of it courses through me, and I fight at the tears coming. "She gets to be with him because she's pushy? And skinny. And perfect." The tears begin to gain ground, and I'm in no position to stop them.

Drew frowns. "I wouldn't say perfect. Skinny, yes. Perfect? Calle, this is Amber. This is the girl who, in eighth grade, managed to get her hair stuck in her own locker and then forget the combination. But rather than have anyone cut her hair—just at the end—she waited four hours for someone to come cut the lock off. Four hours. She's pretty damn focused. She's always been insane about Sam Atkins. If anything, admire her stamina. He's the dumbass who can't tell her no."

I take a shaky breath. "She should give seminars. How to harass someone into being with you."

Quietly, Drew says, "Maybe Eli should take it."

The words sting, but they stop the tears. "What's your point, Drew? I should be with Eli even if I don't feel that way about him?" The bell rings for class, and students start to file into the small alleyway between the buildings where we are standing.

"No. It makes more sense than you and Sam Atkins, but no." He stops. He's clearly already said more than he meant to, and now we have an audience. Drew, unlike many of the other actors, only likes an audience when he's in control. "I have to get to class or I'll be late. Don't forget we have lunch rehearsal today."

"Right." I wipe at my wet eyes. "You're real worried about tardiness."

He digs his hands into the front pocket of his Billabong sweatshirt and turns to go. The sweatshirt says "BONG" in big orange letters. For sure, his first-period teacher will make him turn it inside out. Funny, Drew's always willing to push confrontation about things that don't really matter.

. . .

At lunch, I don't go to rehearsal; instead, I walk out behind the gym to the empty, cold football field. My mind is full. Sam. Eli. My fight with Drew. My father in jail. My mother's lies.

The stadium hibernates, a massive sleeping bear. I walk one whole loop around the track before I notice the lone figure crammed into the lower corner of the bleachers. On the visitors' side.

Sam.

He nods when he sees me see him and gives a small wave. I hesitate, then decide to join him.

"Hey." His hands are crammed into the pockets of his grandfather's letterman jacket. Next to him sits an empty plastic Pepsi bottle and a crumpled brown lunch sack.

"What are you doing out here?" I ask.

He smiles slightly. "Hiding from Amber. She won't come out here. Too cold."

I cram my own freezing hands into the pouch of my sweatshirt. "You weren't doing too much hiding this morning in front of the library."

He flushes, staring out at the wintry stretch of field. "You saw that?"

"I'm surprised Yard Duty doesn't start charging you by the hour."

He takes his hands from his pockets and runs them through his hair. "I'm sorry about that." He looks sideways at me, but I won't catch his eye. I stare at the cement floor of the stadium, the gray amoebas of smashed gum, the faded illegible graffiti. He says, "I guess we're sort of together now."

"I guess you are." I can smell the undercut of salt in the chilly air. Overhead, the sky shifts and churns, the clouds thick like taffy. I feel one or two tiny drops, fairy kisses, on my face.

"Well, whatever makes you happy." I stand quickly. His nearness drains me, and I feel a sudden kinship to his empty soda bottle.

He looks flustered. "You're leaving?"

"Yep." I take the stairs quickly down to the track, fumbling with my Walkman. If I can only get my earphones on, I won't have to listen to all the emptiness.

"Calle?"

My earphones halfway on, I turn to see him standing several feet behind me on the stairs. "What?"

"I don't want it to be like this."

"Like what?"

He shrugs. Sighing, I look at him, bundled there in baggy jeans and his grandfather's jacket. He looks small instead of strong. Maybe Drew was right. Maybe Sam Atkins isn't the type of guy who can say no to a girl like Amber. But if that's true, then he certainly can't handle a girl like me. A girl whose mother remarries more often than other mothers redecorate and whose father maybe left, and for sure was in jail, and who doesn't know her at all. That would be too much for a boy like Sam Atkins.

This is what I tell myself.

"I have rehearsal," I tell him, plugging up my ears with my music, and I leave him there on the stairs.

CHAPTER 15

HEAVY THINGS

...the oddly perky Phish on the stereo, I watch through the curtained window as Ted speeds his red Mustang away down the street, the blond woman next to him hurriedly tying a scarf around her hair. My brown-haired mother remains, crumpled like a napkin on the wedge of grass by the mailbox, having just thrown the empty plastic garbage can after them... and missing...

I HAVE WALKED IN ON a fight, even if they are doing their best to disguise it. The air is thick with it.

"Hi, sweetie," my mom says, placing a bowl of tiny green peas in the center of the table. Her voice is strained, and her eyes never leave Rob who is running water into glasses, his back to me.

"Hi." I glance from her to him. "What's up?"

"Dinner is up!" She is overdoing it. "Spaghetti and veggies, yum!"

"No meatballs," Rob says quietly, still filling glasses at the tap.

My mother's fake smile wavers as her eyes flit to him. "I made the spicy sauce you like," she tells me, placing a bowl of noodles by the peas as she sits down.

Rob places glasses of water on the table. Sitting, he unfolds his napkin into his lap. His eyes down, he spoons peas onto his plate. I notice that the top of his hair is starting to thin, just barely. He does a good job of hiding it.

I pull out my chair and slide into the seat next to my mother. They avoid each other's eyes. Frowning, I spoon myself noodles and sauce, and sprinkle grated Parmesan from the tall green can. We focus on the clink of our forks against the plates, the sound of swallowing.

"How was school?" My mother takes a small bite of pasta and dabs at her mouth with her napkin. She is the only person who can make eating spaghetti a delicate affair. Rob and I both slurp our noodles.

"Fine. I got an A on my math test."

"Good, good," Rob says, attempting a smile in my direction— a fractured, lank smile almost masked by the smear of sauce on his mouth.

My mom catches his eye and points to his mouth. "Sauce," she whispers, which is ridiculous as I can obviously hear her.

Sighing, he reaches for his napkin. After a few strokes, he manages to get most of it. My mom wrinkles her nose. She tries to point out the last stray bit, using her own face as a map. "A little on the left side…"

"Oh, for *christsake, Alyson!*"

My fork clatters to the plate, and my mother freezes as if she's been struck. I have never heard Rob yell. From the look of my mother's face, she hasn't either.

He stands abruptly. "Can I just eat my goddamn food?" He picks up his plate and leaves the room. The door to their bedroom bangs shut. Soon we can hear their small TV click on.

My mother takes a sip of water, dabs her mouth, and eats a forkful of peas. I wait.

And wait. Finally, I ask, "Well?"

"It's really nothing."

I look down the hallway toward their door. "That didn't seem like nothing."

She chews slowly, eyeing me. Swallowing carefully, she says. "Adults just fight sometimes is all."

"I'm not nine."

Sighing, she pushes her peas around on her plate with her fork. Then dropping her voice, she says, "It's mostly a money thing."

"Like we don't have any?" I ask.

She nods. "The job is not going the way he expected it to. And his boss is putting a lot of pressure on him."

I realize that I still have no idea what Rob does for a living, which is sort of embarrassing. I decide that I won't admit this to her.

"Can you pick up more hours at the shop?" My mom doesn't really like working at OM! She hates retail, but she gets a great discount on the clothes. Discount is my mother's favorite word.

"I can barely get three eight-hour shifts now," she confides. "Business is really slow. Kelly had to cut Jason's hours too. I should go back to school. We can't live on eight bucks an hour."

Every time we have a financial crisis, my mother talks about going back to school. I don't really know why she says "back" since she never started in the first place.

"Why don't you waitress again?" I finish the last of my peas and spoon more from the bowl. They're cold, but I'm starving, and no one else seems to want seconds.

She shrugs. My mother's a terrible waitress and she knows it, but it paid better than eight bucks an hour.

"I could get a job," I offer. I have no idea what I'd do, maybe baby-sit or get a job at one of the local restaurants. "It's almost winter break. People need holiday help."

"No way," she says quickly. "You need to study. You're going to college."

"Mom, I can work and still go to college. School is not hard."

"You're only a freshman," she says. "It just gets harder and harder."

I'm only slightly ashamed at how quickly I back down from my offer. If I push her, she'd let me get a job at a bookstore or somewhere else reasonably educational. But I don't really want to work—it would take too much time away from drama stuff—so I just nod and eat my peas.

"Anyway," my mother says, as if she's finishing an internal conversation out loud, "I'm sure it's nothing; it's just a bit rocky at work for him."

With a swift opening of the bedroom door, Rob appears in the doorway. "I'll be out." He doesn't wait for an answer. Pulling on a jacket, he leaves.

Something cold, fear maybe, trickles through me, and the peas sit hard in my belly. What if we have to move again? I voice my concern, careful not to sound as freaked out as I suddenly feel.

"Oh, no," my mom assures me, reaching across the table to close her hand over mine, her eyes resting sadly on the recently closed front door. "We won't move. It's not that serious." This last comment sounds hollow and unsure of itself—her eyes not at all behind her words.

CHAPTER 16
SHOOT THE MOON

...I give the Norah Jones CD to Mom for Christmas, and she plays it in the new CD player that Dan bought her. Our Christmas tree glows in the pale light of the foggy Sacramento morning, strung with white lights and blue ornaments like Mom saw in the Pottery Barn catalog. Dan reads by the fire, covered in the apple-red fleece blanket I got him, and Mom bakes cookies in the kitchen. The house is warm smells of cinnamon, and the recently unwrapped presents are stacked about in piles. I sit in the center of the room, in the middle of a mound of wrinkled wrapping paper, and smell and watch and drink it all in...

I MAKE IT THROUGH AN entire English class without looking at Drew. I got to class early and buried my head in a book so I didn't have to watch him walk in. We still haven't spoken since the Sam and Amber show (as Sara likes to call it) debuted last week in front of the library. Mr. Ericson's been on a lecture stint so we haven't done any group work, which makes it easier.

At the bell, Drew sprints for the door, but Alexa waits as I stuff my books in my backpack. Luckily, Mr. Ericson didn't notice that I spent the duration of his lecture doing my math homework. We're reading *Lord of the Flies*, which I read last summer anyway.

"You two should talk," Alexa says, slinging her maroon corduroy bag over her shoulder. "You'll have to do it. Drew can be really stubborn." I don't respond. She shrugs and adjusts her bag. "Apparently he's not the only one," she says under her breath but loud enough.

"Calle?" Mr. Ericson is standing behind his lectern.

"Yeah?"

He looks at Alexa quickly, clears his throat, and looks back at me. "Umm. Can I talk to you for a second?"

Alexa raises her eyebrows. "I'll see you at lunch," she says. "Bye, Mr. E."

"Bye, Alexa." He watches her leave the room before his eyes slip back to me. I wait. Finally, he says, "Listen, I wanted to talk to you."

"Okay."

He comes out from behind the lectern to lean against the table where we turn our homework into the "In" box and pick it up from the "Out" box. "I'm a bit worried about your performance in class."

He *had* seen me doing my math homework. "I'm sorry about the math, Mr. Ericson. I just got a little behind."

He frowns slightly—okay, he didn't see the math homework and is clearly talking about something else. I want to kick myself for offering information I didn't need to give.

He sidesteps it. "I mean your English work. It's slipping a little. The in-class essay you wrote on the poetry unit was not up to your standards."

"Oh," I say, looking at my shoes, knowing that the essay had been crap. I had spent most of that period thinking about my fight with Eli and trying not to watch Amber and Sam pass notes back and forth. "What did I get?"

"It's not about the grade, Calle." He clears his throat again. "Look, you're the best writer in this class asleep. You and Cass Gordon are probably the best writers in the whole freshman class. You're getting an A. It's just the work itself. It's not what you're capable of."

Cass Gordon? He let her name slip so easily, just a casual mention, not really the point of what he's saying at all, but it hits me and I can't hear what else he's saying. When does Cass Gordon write? She never even comes to school. I try to focus. He's still talking, and I haven't heard any of it. Finally, when I clearly should have said something, he stops, looking closely at me. "Is everything okay?"

I look at his face. Some teachers pry, but he seems genuinely concerned. I notice the small, spider-web wrinkles around his gray eyes; he must be older than I thought. "No," I say quietly.

"Do you want to talk about it?" He folds his arms across his chest. "Maybe I can help?"

"I doubt it."

"Try me."

Before I can stop myself, I tell him all about my dad, even pull the letter from my backpack.

"So I can't even contact him," I finish, jamming the letter back into the front pocket.

He softly whistles. "That's a lot to deal with."

He doesn't know the half of it. Besides my dad, there's my mom and her downhill slide with Rob, my fight with Eli, and the one with Drew. Alexa's annoyed with me, and to top it off, Sam and Amber are making out all over campus. I can't escape them. It's like they figure out where I'll be and then set up make-out camp. But to Mr. Ericson, I just say, "Yeah."

"Have you talked more with your mom about it?" When I shrug as an answer, he argues the point. "You know, I spoke with your mom at Back to School Night. She seems easy to talk to."

I try to explain that she *is* easy to talk to. She just doesn't want me talking to my father. "He was a mistake for her, so she assumes he'll be a mistake for me. She's totally weird about him."

"Well, he clearly hurt her." Something dark slips behind his eyes. I notice his cords, his soft tan sweater, the gray in the dark hair at his temples. No wedding ring. "I know something about that," he says. I study the posters on the wall. Noticing my discomfort, he changes the subject. "You should talk to her. I'm sure she has good reasons why she doesn't want you talking to your dad."

I frown. "She doesn't. It's all about her," I tell him. "I mean, Mr. Ericson, if it was your daughter, you'd want to be able to see her, right?"

He hesitates and then pulls a yellow brick of sticky notes from his pocket and writes down some information. "You know there's a search program online that helps you locate people. Maybe you could try it." Unpeeling the top note, he hands it to me. "Here. My sister's husband found a cousin he hadn't seen in years."

I look at the website information, my mind racing. "Thanks."

"Sure."

The bell rings. We've talked away the whole twenty-five-minute lunch period. Mr. Ericson has a brown sack on his desk. I can only imagine a plastic-wrapped sandwich inside and an apple, maybe some cookies. "You didn't even get to eat," I worry.

He waves the thought away. "I have prep sixth period. I'll eat then. What about you? Do you want me to write you a pass to the cafeteria?"

"No thanks," I tell him. "I'll just eat my sandwich between classes." I don't actually have a sandwich, but I don't want him offering me his—even his imaginary one. Besides, I'm not very hungry during school lately.

"Okay." He moves back around behind his lectern. "Well, thanks for the talk. Have a good break."

"Sure." I leave the room. I'm all the way out of the little hallway and halfway across the quad before it dawns on me that I should have been thanking him.

• • •

Today, a clear sky peeks through tissue-paper clouds. After breakfast, I grabbed my song journal and walked to the ocean. The beach stretches, blinking at the bright winter light like a cat awakened suddenly when the sun appears from behind a tree. This morning, my mom went for a long walk. The past few days she's been pale with dark circles staining the skin beneath her eyes.

Today, when she got home, she seemed better, rosy cheeked and crammed full of endorphins. Humming an Aimee Mann song over and over, she made Rob and me mounds of scrambled eggs and soy bacon (which, I have to admit, wasn't as bad as I thought it'd be). Rob has been sullen, running a lot and prone to long stretches with the TV in the bedroom, but this morning—with the light spilling through the kitchen window, I felt things creak into place. Settle. He even left late for work, lingering with us at the table.

The first weekend I met Rob, he made us breakfast. Mickey Mouse pancakes, even though I was fourteen. I remember how his face fell when the chocolate-chip eyes melted into running puddles so that Mickey resembled a tearful drag queen. My mother laughed until orange juice spurted from her nose. Watching Rob, I knew he would fall in love with her. Even with orange juice out her nose, my mother was radiant.

We have two weeks off from school for winter break, and I have nothing planned. I spent the weekend helping Ms. Hecca clean out the costume barn. Yesterday, I heard three songs that sparked memories, and I only had time to jot notes. Today, with a whole unplanned Monday of no school before me and with the sun on my face, I will fill out the bodies of these skeletal notes, give them color and shape.

I bite the end of my pen, the black Bic top pliable in my teeth, and look at the water. What is it about water that frees me? Down on the thin strip of beach, a man throws a ball for a dog that becomes a white blur in the chase of it. When the dog pauses to scoop the ball from the waves, I smile at the perfect hoop of black around his eye and the one bent ear that just won't stand up straight. We've never had a dog—my mother claims allergies—and I have always wanted one. A smooth head to run my hand over, a wagging tail at the end of the day.

I slip on my headphones, letting Tori Amos narrate the view.

"Hey, Calle." A voice through my headphones, a hand touching my shoulder.

I start, dropping my pen in the loose sand at the base of the bench. Looking up, Sam is part sun, part sky. My stomach roils with the memory of our first walk here.

"Sorry." He bends to pick up my pen. "I didn't mean to scare you."

"It's okay." I snap my journal shut and turn off my music.

"You writing?" He wears a cotton sweater the deep burnt orange of a Halloween pumpkin; it brings out the copper in his hair. His jeans are faded and fraying at the edges. I can't take it all in. Instead, I look down at my journal and nod.

He says, "Can I bother you?"

"Sure. I mean…no bother." I'm wearing a San Diego State sweatshirt my mother found at Goodwill and a pair of thick, grungy sweats that Rob gave me. I don't even bother to try to fix my hair, but I'm happy that I've been sucking on peppermint Life Savers for the past hour.

He sits next to me. "I went to your house. Your mom said you were here."

I take in both statements. He has seen my house. He has met my mom. I'm not sure which one worries me more.

He decides for me. "She's really pretty, your mom."

"Yeah. Clearly, it's not genetic." I attempt a laugh, but it comes out more like a hiccup.

"Shut up," he nudges me, all boy, all football player, and almost knocks me off the bench. "Oh, sorry." He grabs my arm and rights me.

I brush a toppled lock of hair out of my eyes. "It's okay."

"What are you listening to?"

"Tori Amos. 'A Sorta Fairy Tale,'" I say. The first time at this beach with Sam felt like a fairy tale. Not anymore. Fairy tales are only good for the lead characters. And I didn't get to be the princess in this one. At best, I got to be the frog. The frog that doesn't transform after the kiss. Who just sits there on the log eating flies. No one wants to be that frog.

"That's a great song." He folds his hands in his lap. Clears his throat twice. At first, I think he's going to explain why he's here, but he just watches the sun on the waves.

Finally, he says, "It's beautiful today. My dad says days like this in December make the housing prices in California worth it."

"Yeah," I agree, knowing only that the housing prices are so far out of our range that I have no need to know what they are.

"You're probably wondering what I'm doing here." He looks sideways at me.

"A little bit, sure." I slide back on the bench so that my feet come off the ground. Whoever built this bench must have been six-five. I swing my legs slightly back and forth; then, realizing this might be obnoxious, I tuck them cross-legged under me.

"I needed to talk to you," he says. "You sure ran off the other day at the stadium."

He's seen me every day in school since. I'm not exactly hard to reach. "Yeah. I had rehearsal."

He nods. "You building the set again?"

"Yeah."

"The fall play was really good. I liked what you did with the set."

"That was Alexa. I just fill it in." He did not come to the beach to tell me he liked the set. Tiny bubbles of impatience pop in my stomach.

Perhaps sensing this, he says, "I'm really sorry about Amber. I should have told you."

Told me that he's seeing her, that he loves her, that she stalks him and he's thinking about getting a restraining order? I say, "Okay."

"We've been kind of on and off since seventh grade." He clears his throat again but doesn't continue.

"Drew told me."

"Oh?" He looks at me curiously. "What did he say?"

"That you've been on and off since seventh grade."

He nods, agreeing with his own statement. "We have."

"I believe you."

"She's a nice girl," he starts.

More bubbles, bigger, angrier ones, swell in me. "Hmm, that's interesting." My voice is sharp edged, serrated sharp.

He sighs. "You're mad."

"Not mad," I say, clearly mad.

"I don't want you to be mad." He bites his lip, his face a mix of worry and hurt. Fear?

The largest of the bubbles pops. "What do you want me to say, Sam? That I'm happy for you? That I think it's great you're with

Amber? Do you need to not feel guilty? Don't feel guilty, okay? So we kissed. It's not a big deal. I don't need to hear this. I have a lot going on too. I can be the frog."

"What?" He looks just worried now.

I decide not to explain it to him. "Nothing."

"Your mom told me that things are hard for you right now, that you're upset about her and your stepdad fighting a lot."

"My mother has a big mouth."

"I know what it's like to have things going on at home," he continues, turning sideways to look at me. "I don't want to add to that."

"I'm fine." I study the corduroy cover of my journal.

"I mean, things are hard for me too, you know. That's why… that's why I just need to be with Amber right now. She sort of gets the history."

"That's fine. Whatever. I'm fine."

He stares at the hypnotic thumb that I'm running back and forth over the cover of my journal. "I don't think you are."

"I wish you'd just go," I tell him, opening my journal to a blank page. "I'm writing."

"I wish you'd talk to me." He touches the side of my face.

I brush his hand away. "Don't." I start to write nothing in my journal. I describe the sky, the water, the sand, willing him to leave by the sheer force of racing the pen across the page. Finally, he sighs, tells me to have a nice break, and leaves.

When I'm sure he's a good distance away, I look up from my scrawl and watch his retreating back, the orange sweater, his washed jeans the color of the ocean. Even in the warmth of the day, I shiver, my tears cold on my face.

• • •

Winter break passes. A Christmas tree goes up, then down. I listen to music and go to some movies with Alexa and Drew. I search Google and Yahoo People for Jake Winter. There are two in California, so I call both numbers. One guy is a doctor. I call the number anyway. A little girl answers the phone, and I hear laughing in the background. I hang up without saying anything. The other number is disconnected. A couple of musicians turn up, but they are all from the East Coast. I even try to find jail records, but nothing comes up. Either he's not out there, or I'm just lousy at finding things.

My mother and Rob take me to Greta's Diner for my fifteenth birthday on New Year's Eve before they go to a party at Rob's office. I eat chicken soup and think of Eli. His visit to my house. His joke about the chicken and the French chef that I can never remember but that makes me laugh.

I do not talk with my mom about my father.

• • •

The first day back at school, I push open the thick glass doors of the Little Theatre and walk into darkness. Only the footlights glow at the base of the stage. Confused, I check my watch. Three-thirty. I'm on time for rehearsal, but no one else is. Considering most of the drama kids live in the theater, I check my watch again.

Footsteps echo on the empty stage. Looking up, I see Eli walk across, carrying a paper coffee cup from a nearby café. He stops and looks around, his confusion mirroring mine.

"Hey," he says, spotting me. He takes a short drink from the sippy lid, and comes down the middle staircase and up the aisle. "What's the scoop? Rehearsal's three-thirty, right?"

"I thought so."

"We should check Hecca's office," he says, passing by me toward the back of the room. Ms. Hecca has a tiny windowed-in office just off the lighting booth where she posts rehearsal schedules and flyers for plays in the city or at the community college.

"It's at five-thirty," Eli calls back. "Heck's got some sort of emergency. I better call my parents. I was supposed to work at the restaurant tonight." He flips open his cell phone and starts dialing.

I join him at her office. On the door is posted a sign lettered in Hecca's large, swelled writing:

Sorry, guys! Emergency.
We'll have rehearsal today
at 5:30 SHARP! Kisses–H.

Eli closes his phone and takes a sip of coffee. "Maybe I can just set lights early," he suggests, avoiding my eyes.

"Sure." I walk away from the office and sit in one of the back theater seats. Outside, it has started to rain, erasing a four-day stretch of January sun. Through the smoky glass of the theater, the world is a swirl of gray. The lights on the stage snap on. I squint at the blinding white wash.

"Sorry," Eli says through the speakers. The lights fade to blue; with the rain streaming down the window, we could be underwater.

The winter show, a festival piece Hecca wrote, opens in two weeks, and the set is nearly finished. The play is set in a fairy-tale world, and Alexa designed a large storybook whose pages turn for the six scene changes. We've been laboring over the canvas all week, at times frustrated with the lumpy un-fairytale-like quality of our images.

But with the wash of Eli's lighting design, the blues and the ambers and the pale reds, the pages come alive. Alexa spent yesterday threading silvery strands of paint for accent—an accent I couldn't see until now that the scenes are bathed in stage light.

"Wow," Eli breathes, sliding in next to me. "It looks awesome."

Eli is the only person I know besides my mom who says "awesome," and I love it about him. "Thanks. Alexa's so talented."

"Not just Alexa," he says.

My face burns, and I'm glad he has the lights on low wash so that I'm currently in shadow. "It looks good because of your lighting. Especially the moon."

Alexa and I made a five-foot moon and suspended it from the ceiling on fishing line. Although two-dimensional, with Alexa's creamy shading and Eli's clever spotlight, the moon looms full bodied in the air above the stage.

He shrugs. "That moon was a great idea." He knows the actual idea of the moon was mine, and I smile. I don't deserve Eli. We haven't talked for weeks. Before break, he avoided my eyes; during break, he was in Hawaii with his parents. His kiss seems far away in another world. Now, I just want to be near him. He smells like rain and coffee.

"I don't think any fairy tale is complete without a moon," I tell him. "Moons are so lonely and hopeful." I sit up straighter, feeling silly. The light in the room, the quiet rain, have induced a trance. "I guess that's sort of stupid."

"No, it's not," he says quickly. "I think the whole play is sort of lonely and hopeful. I hope it's good, that people like it."

"They will."

"Today's our first day with partial costumes," he says. "It should be fun to see the whole thing coming together."

"I'm just looking forward to seeing you in a bunny suit."

He laughs. Hecca has Eli as the White Rabbit from *Alice in Wonderland*. He's sort of half-narrator, half-character in the play. "Um. I'm a rabbit, thank you very much."

"Sorry. Rabbit suit."

He sighs as we watch the light on the stage. Then, he says, almost in a whisper, "I'm sorry about…about the thing at your house."

I shake my head, knowing we've already moved past it. "You shouldn't be sorry, Eli. I'm the one who ran you out of there. You're the sweetest person I know. I don't deserve you."

"That's true," he says, and I swat him lightly with the cuff of my sweatshirt.

"Anyway, I hope we're friends," I say.

"Now you're being stupid." But he seems to swell with it, our clearing this hurdle in our friendship. He stands. "I better check the second-act lights—make sure we don't have any shadows." As he stands, a human shadow moves outside the window. I look in time to see Cass disappear around the corner.

"What the hell?" Eli goes to the window, looking after her. "What was she doing here?"

I shrug. "What's her deal?" I try to sound casual.

"You don't know?"

"I mean, I know she's a loner or whatever, but why is she like that?"

Eli climbs over the row of theater seats, sitting on the top of one of the chairs and planting his green-leather Converse-clad feet where his butt should be. Hecca would kill him if she saw him sitting in the chair like that.

He sighs. "Cass's got a totally screwed-up family. She doesn't have a dad. Her mom's a fugitive."

"What?"

Eli nods. "Seriously. She's, like, wanted by the FBI. Cass never sees her mom. She lives with her uncle over on Sanderson Street. He owns that bar—Lucky's."

"Whoa," I breathe. Maybe Cass and I have more in common than I thought.

"I'm surprised you didn't know. It's a small town. Word gets around."

"What'd her mom do?"

"She's some activist or something. And I heard that, like, twenty years ago she was with a bunch of people who blew something up, something major. I mean, a guy died in it."

"Seriously?" The word catches slightly in my throat and comes out staggered, airless.

He shakes his head. "Yeah, I know. It's wild. Like something out of a movie or something."

"Whoa," I say again.

"Yeah." He looks out toward where Cass had been a dark flash outside the window. Was she looking for me?

Sara comes walking across the stage, sucking a lollipop. She extracts it and points it at us. "Hey!" she says. "You two made up! Eli, don't sit in the chair like that."

"Okay, Mom." He slides into the seat.

She waggles the lollipop at us. "This is so great. If you two stayed mad for the show, I would have had a nervous breakdown or something."

Eli, fond of Sara's exaggerations, winks at me. "Now your nervous breakdown will have to be about something else," he tells her. She sticks out her tongue, green from the lollipop.

"Pretty," Eli says.

"Oh, my god!" she shrieks, turning to see the set. "The moon looks incredible. Oh my god, this is going to be the best play we've ever done here."

Of course, Sara says this about every play. Smiling, I gaze at the glowing white moon, and, hanging there bathed in light and shadowed with lonely sweeps of silver paint, it gazes back.

CHAPTER 17
PEOPLE TALKIN'

...cars snake up the mountain, their taillights rows of red glowing eyes in the darkness. With all of the headlights beamed forward, the mountain and the gash of sky behind shine faintly purple. My mother sings quietly to the Lucinda Williams song on the radio and inches forward in the car. All of the spiritual people have come to Sedona to sit on the mountain and commune with the energy. Mom says a little spiritual energy in our life couldn't hurt...

THE NOTE IS A POEM, puzzling and strange. After PE today, I find it crammed into the edge of my gym locker. The writing looks knifed onto the page in thick black marker, but the words, locked together in crisp staccato, are music.

> Words, hurled as whispered bombs,
> Trap, attack, hack at your soul
> Until you fall back into the darkness,

Into the hanging arms of a stranger,
Kicking and biting, crying, knowing
You will never be home again, never
Find home at the end of that strange,
Familiar road you've always walked
Softly on. The bombs are buried deep
In the soil of our hearts, our heads, our dreams—
But you slip, you clutch the whisper
That's not a bomb, a crutch, that's lurking under
The wind, the waves, the breaking glass of trust,
That hovers, like a waiting fox, in the corner
Of your eye to guide you, to hide you from the
Darkness. Only this fox, this curled silent sadness,
Needs you more than you need *him*.
Don't be fooled by fools.
Meet at Lucky's tonight at 8. For Sam.

Outside, in the shallow, wet air that promises rain tonight, I tuck the note deep into the front pocket of my jeans and decide on which of the dozen lies racing through my mind I will tell my mother.

. . .

The road to Lucky's is not well lighted. I have a few street lamps but no yellow squares of lit windows to guide me. I stuff my hands, already gloved, into the front pocket of my sweatshirt and wish a flashlight would appear in the dark air in front of my eyes. No such luck.

I told my mother that I was going to the movies with Alexa and Drew. Distracted, she gave me a little wave but did not look up from the onions she was chopping at the kitchen counter. Since any announcement of movie-going usually results in a full-fledged interrogation—What movie? What is it rated? What is the running time?—her small wave and lack of eye contact surprised me. Something is wrong with her lately. Still, I was lying to her, so I guess her distraction was in my favor. She didn't even give me a curfew.

I stumble down Sanderson Street, straining my eyes against the shadows. The few scattered street lamps give out a smudgy light. The sound of the ocean grows louder with each deserted block I pass. As I walk, I pass some boarded-up buildings and a few vacant lots, and then I come upon a stretch of train tracks that have clearly not been used in years. Even so, I look both ways before stepping across them, navigating my way around broken bottles, candy and condom wrappers, and a blue running shoe.

I hear music under the crash of waves before I see any place that could be producing it. Soon, though, hovering in the distant dark appears a ripple of red neon, a sign that becomes legible only when I am standing directly in front of it: Lucky's.

I extract my hands from my pockets and study the outside of the bar. Below the cherry Slurpee red of the sign is a blank cement block of a building, which would undoubtedly be gray in the light of day.

Rain starts, a light mist on my face that clings to my eyelashes and cheeks. Not wanting to look too much like a drowned rat, I hurry inside.

Jingle bells ring the door, either left a month after Christmas or always there, but no one looks up as I enter. The light is as dim as the doorway outside, and the place smells of old cigarettes, grease, and something sharper and unidentifiable.

A sign that reads: "No Persons Under 21 Permitted" hangs faded by the inside of the door. Someone has crossed out the "1" with heavy blue pen but the number still shows faintly beneath the ink. Low country music infuses the room.

There are four or five people at the bar—all men, all shoulders and raincoats, with beer glasses in varying stages of empty. A man eyes me from behind the counter, and my heart beats erratically. In no way could I pass for twenty-one.

"You looking for Cass?" His voice is surprisingly low and soft, awkward in the sandpaper edges of his face.

"Yes," I manage.

He nods to the back of the bar, a smattering of tables and an elevator-sized stage set with a single chair and microphone. Several people sit at the tables. Barely visible from the door, crammed into a corner table, are Cass and Sam. They are whispering quietly, sodas half finished in front of them. Cass looks up and notices me.

"Hey." She waves me over.

Sam turns his head and sees me, and the surprise that seizes his features is not quickly masked. He, clearly, did not get a note in his PE locker. His gaze darts back to Cass, but she is standing, sliding her chair in.

"You want a Coke?" she asks.

"Sure."

She goes behind the bar, her motions familiar, scooping ice and spurting soda from a tube into the glass. She pauses and looks at me. "You want cherry in it?"

"No thanks."

I stuff my hands into the pockets of my raincoat and stare at the wall behind Sam's head, trying not to notice his lack of eye contact. He studies the table, sips his drink, and runs his finger through the rings of moisture his glass has left.

"Here." Cass plunks the soda onto the table. "Sit down," she says, her normally gruff voice softened.

I sit where she had been sitting since there are only two chairs at the table.

"I have to work," she tells us, and disappears through a swinging door next to the bar.

"So you know Cass?" Sam asks, his eyes settling on me for the first time.

I sip my Coke. "We have PE the same period."

He nods and swirls the ice in his drink. "She's a good person," he says after a minute.

"Seems so."

"People think she's a freak but she's not." The music in the room is suddenly shut off mid-song and, though the music was low, its absence creates a hollow, empty feel to the bar.

"How do you know her?" I ask.

Cass reemerges through the swing of the door. She has pulled her hair into a ponytail and removed her sweatshirt. She wears a

132

black shirt that says "GIRL," and her studded black belt balances her baggy army cargo pants precariously on her hips.

I wait for Sam's answer, but he just watches her as she steps onto the small stage, moves the chair, and adjusts the microphone.

"Is she going to sing?" I ask, surprised.

"Not really," Sam says.

"Good evening, folks," she says into the microphone, her voice clear and strong. The casual buzz of conversation at the tables stops, and the men at the bar swivel in their seats to watch her.

I am struck by the strangeness of her clear voice, her straight shoulders. At school, she is ghost-like, the shadow of a storm cloud. Here she is neither ghost nor shadow.

"I thought it was time for a little spoken word," she says, to a sprinkling of applause from some of the tables. "I wrote some new ones for tonight's performance."

Performance? I look at Sam, who is watching her, chin in hand.

She speaks, low lidded, into the microphone. "This first one is about identity. Most of you went to AB High, so you know a little something about having this spelled out to you by a bunch of bastards who don't know anything about you." The tables cheer and applaud, hands over heads. Sam whistles through his teeth.

She puts her hand around the stem of the microphone. "It's called…'YOU.'"

Then she begins.

> YOU see me each day, YOU with your yellow cello-
> phane eyes

Blind to the clarity of what is me, of what is under the
tough of my skin,
YOU with your varnished truth, your shoe-shined words
that scuff
And cut me. That carve me up and break me into tiny
puzzle pieces
Of lies.
Don't look at me. You don't see what you think you see.

I have heard only a few spoken-word poems before, some of Ani
DiFranco's and a short movie clip Mr. Ericson showed us during
the poetry unit, but they were not like seeing it live. Throughout
the piece, Cass becomes every word, her body swaying, her arms
punctuating, her voice both accusatory and sympathetic.

She finishes:

And YOU with your Oedipus eyes, with your gold-plated
lies,
YOU won't wrap me, package me, trap and fasten me to
who you MAKE me—daily.
To who I have to be so YOU can be who you think
YOU are.
Even though,
In the dark decay of your soul, you know you aren't
That girl, that boy, that face, that smile that disgraces the
loneliness
You hold down, down under the black water of your heart,

The loneliness
That knows that even as it gasps for air,
YOU are losing your hold on it; we're ALL losing our
hold on it,
And it has only to wait minutes more for the clean
honest air
To fill its lungs with success, for it to beat us,
Defeat us, forever.

She closes her eyes, nods into the microphone, and says, "Thank you."

After a brief hush and a quick intake of air, the room breaks into applause. I am caught between feeling like I've had ice water dumped down the back of my shirt and like I've taken a punch to the stomach. Even with all of the performances I've seen from Drew and Sara and Eli, nothing has ever hit me like this one, the sheer energy of it pounded into me for two breathless minutes. In those 120 seconds, she transformed the shape of the room.

"Wow," I say. And I suddenly know who the bathroom poet is.

"I know," Sam says, watching as Cass drinks the last of her Coke several steps from the microphone. "She's amazing."

"I just need a refill," Cass tells the audience before dashing to the bar.

"I had no idea she could do that." I drink my Coke, my senses whirling: cold, sweet, bubbles, ice against my lips.

"She's up there every Friday," Sam explains. "This is all the stuff she writes during the week."

I take a deep breath. "You've seen her before?" Somehow the thought of Sam alone at the corner table seems too bizarre.

"A few times." He hesitates, attempting to wipe the wet from the table with a white square of napkin. "When I need to get away."

"From your mom?" If I'm too bold here, he doesn't show it.

"Did Cass tell you about my mom?" He digs an ice cube out of the glass with his finger and chews it.

"Not really," I shrug. "I've heard some things."

"What things?" His eyes darken, immediately guarded.

"That it's alcohol. That she gets sent away."

Red crawls over his face. "It's not alcohol," he says gruffly. "People should keep their mouths shut."

I watch him steadily, hoping my face doesn't betray the ragged beating in my chest. "People need reasons. Explanations. If they aren't given them, they create them." These words echo in my ears. I think of my father, imagine him sitting alone in a jail cell. Wrongly accused. He must have been.

Cass stops by our table, her eyes absorbing my stare and Sam's red face. "Things okay?" she asks, her glass newly filled and fizzing.

"Yeah, sure." Sam looks up at her. "Great."

"You're amazing," I tell her.

A flicker of a smile catches her mouth. "Stick around." She makes her way to the stage.

"It's depression," Sam says, watching Cass set her drink on the chair and fiddle with the microphone. His eyes slip to me. "My mom. Clinical depression. She gets sent away for it."

I want to respond, but Cass is starting her next poem. As the words wash over me, her pulsing, rhythmic anger charging the air, I watch Sam's face and feel the pain there.

. . .

Sam doesn't show up at school for three days. He was in English class Monday, in the hall, by his locker, in the lunch line, with my eyes tracking him like a Sherpa. Then he was gone. No Tuesday. No Wednesday.

Now, Thursday, his plastic seat sits empty in English. Amber hovers around it, her pink-nailed hands curled protectively over the back of the chair.

"He's been calling me like three times a night," she announces loudly to Kandace Jones, a bird-boned fake blond from the cheer-leading squad who never seems to do anything other than fix her makeup and echo whatever Amber says like a parrot.

"Three times," she says, looking up from her chair into Amber's smug face, a mascara wand poised before her compact.

But Amber is not talking to her. She's talking to me. Even from halfway across the room. Her eyes flit occasionally to Kandace's narrow painted face to keep up the façade, but she stares mostly in my direction. I bury my face in my English book, *To Kill a Mockingbird*, which I've read three times already, and will myself not to meet her eyes.

"Family emergency," she says, sighing heavily. "His mom again, poor thing. They took her to a special hospital. In San Francisco."

"San Francisco," Kandace breathes, more impressed, it appears, by the city than by the reason Sam's there.

"Yeah." Amber nods dramatically. "Thank God he has me. I don't know what he'd do if he had to go through this alone."

Alexa rolls her eyes at Drew. "Well, thanks to you now, Amber, and your public service announcement, he has the whole school behind him."

Amber ignores her. Her eyes bore into my skull, but I read the same line over and over, hum a Jack Johnson song under my breath, and don't meet her stare.

CHAPTER 18

BUSTED STUFF

...emerging from my room to the sound of scissors snapping—snick, snick, snick—over the low growls of the Dave Matthews Band. Mom has dumped Ted's remaining clothes in a pile on her right. On her left, she is making another pile: the shredded remains of jeans, shirts, some ties—snick, snick, snick—ribbons of material curl away from the gleaming blades. I watch her for ten minutes, but if she notices me, she never looks up from her work...

THE HOUSE IS DARK. NO one home, I guess. I drop my backpack by the front door and ease out of my jacket. My head spins with Sam's absence, with Amber's English class announcements, with the near end of a long, heavy week that still has a day left in it.

My ears prick at a choking sound from the kitchen, one deep intake of ragged air and a whimper like a puppy. I rush to the doorway, my heart already tipping into familiar fear.

"Mom?"

She is crouched in the dim of the kitchen, wedged into the corner where the cabinets meet. She is shadowed in the filtered light coming through the window, but I see clearly that she's wearing only her bra and a pair of jeans. And that she's sobbing. She clutches a bedroom hanger and a pair of Rob's running shorts. Seeing me, she holds them as if in prayer and says, "All he left," through her sobs.

I pull it all in at once: her tears, the hanger, the shorts, her words, now repeating, "All he left, Calle." I know this scene well. In my heart, I know that I have been waiting for it, each of my days without it just preamble to this—to what always is.

"When did he leave?"

My voice is so low, I can't imagine she's heard me, but in her state, her senses are heightened like a dog's. Her head dips into her chest. "Today. While I was at work."

"He took everything? Did he leave a note?" Sometimes they leave a note; sometimes they just leave.

"Yes." She nods into her chest. I don't know which question she's answering, so I decide to ask them independently. No compound questions for her, not now. She answers: yes, he took everything except, it seems, a pair of running shorts, and no, he did not leave a note.

"Money?"

She shakes her head. I frown. I would have picked Rob for one that would leave money, but you can never tell.

"What happened?" I can hear my voice building, taking on a shrill echo of the hard pulse in my ears. "Mom! Answer me. What happened?"

Her sobs amplify. My body heats. I want her to answer me, to stand up, to put a shirt on.

"Mom. Get up!" I scream. "Get up now!"

She buries her face in the shorts. I have never screamed like this before, and the sound of it startles me. Propels me forward.

I race to the bedroom, my eyes taking in the things missing—the empty closet, the missing pillow, the straight-back chair, the small television. Again. Again. I wrench a battered blue suitcase from the bottom of the closet and yank open my mother's drawers. Tears on my cheeks, I throw in shirts and socks and leggings—anything I can grab hold of.

Returning to the kitchen, I see her on her side, tucked into a ball like a rolly-bug, the kind we flick outside when we find them on the kitchen floor.

"Get up," I say again, my voice harder, less shrill. "We're going to move again, right? That's how this works, right?"

I hurl the suitcase at her, and it splits open, clothes exploding around her. A pair of leggings hooks onto her right foot. She whimpers, face buried in her arms and hair.

Her back is shaking with tears, but I can't stop myself from throwing my words at her. "You can't keep doing this to me! I like it here. I have friends here. This isn't just your life. It's my life too."

She just rocks and rocks.

"Are we moving?" I ask. This is a whisper—almost without air. She doesn't respond, just looks up at me, her eyes liquid and swimming. Afraid. She twists the hanger into a figure eight and rubs her face into the smooth of his shorts. Has she heard any of this?

Probably not. She's too far stuck in the swamp of her own misery, lost back behind vacant eyes. I am just a howling, creeping background noise to her right now. Anger drains away, leaving a dark hollow in me.

"I'll get donuts," I tell her, knowing that this is the only thing I can do right now.

• • •

For a week, my mother slips in and out of agony. Pink Floyd pounds the walls as she moves like a phantom from couch to bed to brown overstuffed chair in the living room, always with the same green fleece blanket wound around her. She doesn't shower; she barely eats (Safeway donut box half full now). Sometimes she cries; sometimes she just stares.

I clean up the suitcase mess in the kitchen. When her work calls, I tell them she is very sick, a horrible flu. On the fourth day, they tell me if she can't produce a doctor's note, she's fired. She produces no note.

I file the bills in order of due date, in order of the ones that I can let lapse and it won't directly affect us. I cancel cable. Fishing my mother's checkbook out of her purse, I pay the electric and water bill. I pull forty dollars out with her ATM card to buy food she picks at without comment. I eat pizza and Kraft dinners, and, once, I make a salad.

I go to school.

I watch Eli and Alexa laughing at lunch, watch Drew abandon his capes for a long, silver trench coat that looks like aluminum foil. They talk about the spring show and what they'll do this summer.

They are fixed in their lives here. I'm such an idiot. I let them get too close; I let them take me in. I can't stop thinking about Sam even if he never even looks at me anymore.

I should have known better.

I sit in English class and ignore Mr. Ericson's concerned looks. Sam is back in class looking thin and tired. Amber fawns on him like a new mother, and he allows it, vacantly. She runs her fingers through his hair, picks imaginary lint off his jacket, and feeds him french fries from a paper tray. Alexa and Drew make gagging noises for my benefit, and for theirs, I try to smile. I don't tell them that my life has disintegrated.

• • •

"Hello?" I tuck the phone between my ear and shoulder, and pull the rest of the laundry from the washing machine.

"Calle?"

"Yeah?"

"It's Rob."

I swallow, my arms full of wet clothes. "Oh." I stuff the clothes in the dryer, freeing a hand to grasp the phone. "Hi." This is a first. The other ones never called.

"Umm…" he pauses. I hear a horn honk, the whine of a distant siren. He must be in his car. "How're things?"

I roll my eyes. "Well, you know what, Rob? They've been better." I push the start button on the dryer.

"Is your mom there?"

I don't know where my mom is. When I got home from school today, she wasn't curled in her usual chair or in bed. "No," I tell him.

"Oh." His car radio plays soft classical music. What road is he driving on? What town is he in now?

He sighs. "Listen, Calle. You're a good kid. It's not fair to you."

It's the most I've ever heard Rob say in one breath. "Don't feel sorry for me, Rob. I've done this before."

"Not that," he says. "You know, she'll never be able to hide completely from him. Not completely. He'll find her. He always does."

What is he talking about? "Who?" I ask, turning and leaning against the rhythmic rocking of the dryer.

On the other end, I can almost hear Rob go pale.

"What are you talking about?" I ask.

"Calle, damn," he says. "Nothing. I'm sorry. I just…tell your mom I'm sorry."

He hangs up.

• • •

"Calle!" calls a voice behind me.

In the midst of my week-long fog, I turn, barely registering him.

Sam stops, catching his breath. He has had to run to catch up to me. "Hey, are you okay?"

I look around at our exposure, the middle of the quad bulging with students eating lunch. "Sure," I say guardedly.

He pauses and looks past me. "It's just you seem upset. You haven't said anything in class all week. I…is…is everything okay?"

"Is everything okay with you?"

His face darkens. "Better now." He pauses. "You going to answer my question?"

Without warning, a tear betrays me.

"Hey." He takes my arm. "What's going on?"

He steers me toward the alleyway between the math and English buildings, away from some stares I've started to attract. The sun doesn't hit here; it is only damp and dirt and shadows. Perfect for us.

I tell him about Rob leaving and watch his features slip into understanding, into worry. I've never told anyone this much before. I stop just short of telling him about Rob's phone call, how strange he sounded. I haven't even told Mom that Rob called—it was too weird, and she's not ready. Besides, in the warm, Tide-scented air of the laundry room, the call didn't even feel real.

"What will you do?" Sam asks, when I seem to have finished.

I shake my head. "I don't know. She lost her job. We can't afford the house." I don't say it out loud, the inevitable. I just say, "We'll do what we always do."

Sam thinks for a minute and seems ready to say something. Then Amber rounds the corner. Always the princess of crappy timing.

"Here you are, Samuel," she says. Her eyes narrow at me, death slits, but she smiles at Sam, an almost computer-generated shift in her features. "Ashley said she saw you come back here. What on earth could you be doing?"

Even though he isn't overly close to me, he takes a shaky step backward. "Calle's upset. We're talking."

She sulks, bottom lip expertly out. "But you were going to help me with math. If I fail Treveli's test, my parents will kill me. And we won't be able to go to Trevor's party."

She coils her arm through his and blinks up at him. I notice that she has a mascara blotch under her eye and a badly covered-up pimple on her chin. Girls like Amber almost never get pimples.

"Oh, right." Sam's gaze slips from Amber to me. "I've got to help her with this test."

"Sure." I wave him away, thankful that the tears have dried by now. "No problem."

Amber whisks him away before he can say anything, leaving me in the alleyway shadows.

Telling him has only emptied me more.

...my mother and I sit on a red blanket on our new living-room floor; she has stopped crying, finally, and her face shines with this next step of our lives, the new walls around us far away from the house we shared with Ted Number 2. A San Diego sun low and warm through the curtainless windows, surrounded by a fortress of boxes, we eat Winchell's donuts, listen to Tracy Chapman, and drink coffee from small white cups...

THE FOLLOWING MORNING, I WAKE to the sound of Ingrid Michaelson on the stereo and the smell of bacon. Bacon! The real stuff—no soy. I throw the covers off and climb out of bed. In the kitchen, my mother has made eggs and bacon and sourdough toast. She sets everything out on the table.

"Morning, sleepyhead," she says cheerily, kissing me on the forehead. She smells of clean jasmine soap and morning air. I notice the Bay View Foods bag. It's only 7:45 a.m. She's been up awhile. Shopping, apparently.

"What's going on?" I rub my eyes and settle into a chair. The bacon is crisp and salty and melts in my mouth. I eat another piece.

"We're moving," she announces, pouring orange juice for us.

The bacon suddenly tastes heavy on my tongue. "What?"

Seeing the look on my face, she rushes on. "Not to another town. To an apartment."

"What are you talking about?"

She takes a bite of toast that she has smeared with grape jelly. "Well, it all happened sort of fast." She dabs at her mouth with her napkin. "You know your friend Sam?"

"Yes." What does he have to do with anything?

"His dad called here. Yesterday. While you were at Drew's."

Drew and I had spent most of the day assembling his photosynthesis project for biology. Finals are next week, and without the project, he won't pass the class. "He called here?"

My mother nods and sips her orange juice. "You'll never believe it. His father offered me a job at Bay View. I start training today."

"He offered you a job?" I'm beginning to sound like Kandace Jones, the parrot cheerleader.

"Yeah. Isn't that great?"

I nod to be encouraging. "It's great." Weird is what I really think it is.

My mom finishes her scrambled eggs. "But we have to move to an apartment. Honey, eat your eggs." She motions to my plate with her fork. "This place is just too expensive on one salary, even a decent one."

I nod again, spooning lukewarm eggs into my mouth. "And you already found one?" Usually we live in the moving van for a few days or a motel. It's never an easy transition. This seems too easy.

"Well, that's the other great thing. Sam's dad owns an apartment complex near the store, and he has a vacancy—an upstairs one. A corner one-bedroom with a study. So you'd still have your own room. It's small, but…"

I interrupt, "You saw it already?"

"Tom—Sam's dad—showed me after the interview yesterday. It's perfect for us. We can move in this weekend." She leans forward, her eyes gleaming. "And get this: Tom knows the landlord here, and he got him to actually pro-rate the rest of our month's rent so we get back our deposit—can you believe it? You certainly know the right people." She drains her orange juice and starts to clear away her plate.

"Mom," I say, handing her my plate as well. "I have finals next week. I have to study."

"I'm sorry, sweetie, but we just can't afford to stay here." She pauses, looking at me from the kitchen. For the first time this morning, her smile falters and her face darkens. "You want to stay here, right? You like Andreas Bay?"

I force my face to brighten. "Yes, of course. It's just so amazing, all at once." I push my chair back and go to her. "Congratulations!" I say, hugging her, breathing in her jasmine smell. I do want to stay here, but something shuts me off and won't let my mother's excitement come in. What's wrong with me?

She pulls away and smiles. "See, Calle. We don't need stupid men in our lives. We can do this on our own."

I agree with her out loud, knowing that without Sam, his dad, and the landlord, we'd be pulling out the battered California map, already bloodied with the red dots of our last residences, and tossing the penny again.

. . .

I close the door to my room, holding the phone with shaky hands. My mother is singing in the kitchen while she washes the dishes that have piled up over the last week. Her first day at her new job was, in her words, "fantastic."

I didn't have the nerve to approach Sam at school today, not with Amber constantly in orbit around him. Now I dial his number. The phone rings twice. He answers.

"Sam?"

"Yeah?"

"It's Calle."

A pause. "Hi."

"I just wanted to thank you. You know, for what you did for my mom." He doesn't say anything right away, so I add, "You didn't have to do that."

"It's no problem. My dad's been looking for someone good for a few weeks anyway. It worked out for him too."

"Yeah, well, it was really nice of you and your dad. He seems like a good guy."

"He's all right." His voice is flat.

After a pause, I say, "Well, I really appreciate it."

"It's no big deal." He sounds like he's covering the speaker on the phone. I hear muffled voices.

"It's a big deal to me."

"Okay," he says awkwardly, his voice suddenly lowering. "You're welcome."

I hear a voice behind him, a low female whisper, a giggle. I realize Amber's at his house. She must have just come into the room.

"I've gotta go," he says quickly, and hangs up.

Stung, I click off the phone and stare at the receiver as if it's the one who's betrayed me.

• • •

The next day, I push open the door to my mom's room and watch her packing. Her back to me, she folds clothes into a cavernous tan suitcase. She hums along to Kelly Clarkson on her stereo.

"Mom?" I step into the room.

"Are you done packing?" She brushes a lock of hair from her eyes and smiles at me.

"Yeah." I don't tell her I keep things ready to go. My folded clothes go into two blue suitcases; the books, CDs, and few stuffed animals have boxes that fit them, boxes I never break down. I've got packing down to a science, so it takes less than an hour.

There are only three posters on my walls: an Ani DiFranco poster of her *Educated Guess* album, a black-and-white Ansel Adams poster of a tree, and an *Alice in Wonderland* print of Alice and the Cheshire Cat.

Alice says, "Would you tell me, please, which way I ought to go from here?"

And the Cat responds, "That depends a good deal on where you want to get to."

Alice says, "I don't much care where..."

The Cat interrupts, "Then it doesn't matter which way you go."

"...so long as long as I get somewhere," Alice says.

"Oh, you're sure to do that," says the Cat. "If only you walk enough."

I love that poser. For obvious reasons.

My mom smiles at me, "If you're done, then you can help me." She hands me a mound of clothes. "Can you fold these?"

I start folding a pair of jeans. "Mom?"

"Hmm?"

"Rob called."

She stops folding and turns to me. "Rob called here?"

I nod. "A while ago."

She raises her eyebrows. "And you didn't tell me?"

I place the jeans in her suitcase and pick up a sweater. "You were..." I pause. "You were kind of out of commission." She flushes and returns to the underwear and panty hose she's untangling from one another. "Mom, he said something kind of weird when he called."

Her head jerks up, her eyes widening. "What? What'd he say?"

"Something like...'He'll find you. He always does.' Something like that. And when I tried to ask him about it, he hung up on me." I avoid her eyes, folding T-shirts. "He's talking about my father, right?"

"Damn." She sits down on the bed, a pair of leggings balled in her hands. "Idiot."

"Rob?"

"Yes, Rob," she sighs.

"What did he mean—he always finds us?" My swollen heart thumps against my chest.

My mom kneads the leggings like bread. "Okay. Don't freak out."

"Don't freak out?"

"Listen, I guess you should know this now."

"Know what?" I wait while she takes a deep breath and lets it out for an impossibly long time. "Know what?" I repeat, annoyance creeping into my voice.

"Your father has been trying to find us for some time, Calle. He's been…well, he's been pretty persistent." She un-balls the leggings and begins folding them in half and then in half again.

"What?" The air in the room seems thick, unbreathable.

The leggings are now a tiny, fat cube of material. She jams them into a nook of the suitcase. "All these times we move…Listen, I want you to know that this has been for your own good. I want you to trust me."

I just stare at her.

"When we've moved…it has been because of the breakups. In a way. Mostly, though, I move us so that he can't find us. I…and I can't say this with enough emphasis…I don't want him in our lives. He gave up that right years ago." She stands and takes a step toward me.

"Are you serious?" Anger surges through me, but I try to put a cap on it. She won't talk if she thinks I'm mad at her. I force my face into surprise, not anger. "I mean, is this for real?"

"Yes."

"He's been trying to find me."

"Yes, but…"

"Mom," I say, stepping back. I need to handle this the right way and not make her defensive, or she won't tell me where he is. "I understand that he hurt you. I really do." I pause, trying to figure out where to go from here. "I know you don't want to see him," I say diplomatically. "But did you ever think that I have a right to know who my father is?"

She nods. "Of course, I did. It's just that, as your mother, I know that he would not be good for you, that he wouldn't treat you the way you're supposed to be treated."

I flare again. What gives her the right to make that decision? "How do you know that?"

"I just know." She returns to the folding, stuffing an oversized sweatshirt into the suitcase.

"But it's not fair."

"Honey, if you knew him…"

"But I don't know him. I'd rather know a bad father than no father at all."

She shakes her head, her eyes sad. "I don't think that's true."

"But…"

"Look, as long as you live with me, you need to respect my choices. I'm sorry, Calle. I'm not budging on this one."

She disappears behind the closet door.

CHAPTER 20
BLIND

...my mother's new boyfriend, Dale, convinces the Napa motel manager to give us an upstairs room so that my mom has a view of the vineyards. I listen to my Train CD through my headphones, bored; my mother smiles at Dale, who gives her a thumbs-up sign. Dale sells cars and gives that same thumbs-up on his local commercials. My mother brushes a short lock of newly blond hair from her eyes and claps her hands together. Dale thinks her new haircut and color make her look like Cameron Diaz. I think they make her look ridiculous...

"THAT TEST WAS BRUTALLY HARD," Drew says, slumping down next to us on the theater stage. "I *hate* biology! What's the point? When are we ever going to need to know that?" He pops open a bag of salt-and-vinegar potato chips.

"Yeah," Alexa says dryly, rolling her eyes at Eli. "Knowing how our bodies function is such a complete waste of time."

"Total waste," Drew says through a mouthful of chips, missing or ignoring her sarcasm.

"Well, I aced my English final," Eli announces, stretching his arms up over his head. "A+."

"Eli, you've never gotten an A+ on anything," Tala teases, slurping noodle soup.

"True," he smiles. "But that's about to change. Oh, oh…" He sits up straighter. "Okay, so…A rabbi, a priest and a monkey walk into a bar." Everybody groans. Eli's smile widens. "So the bartender looks at them and goes, 'What is this? Some kind of joke?'" He beams. "I came up with that during my English final."

Alexa laughs and pats Eli's head. "While you were acing it?" He sticks his tongue out at her. Still laughing, she offers me some carrot sticks. "Brain food."

"Thanks," I say, taking a stick.

"You guys settle in okay?" she asks.

"We did." I say, munching the carrot. The move went smoothly. Alexa, Drew, and Eli helped us move into the new apartment last Saturday. No one seemed to notice that I wasn't speaking to my mother. In fact, I don't think she even noticed. She had tons of food for us: pizza, chips, soda, and a giant silver bowl of M&Ms.

We played music and hauled most of the furniture up the stairs, stuffing it into the tiny rooms. A few chairs went to Goodwill. We donated the couch that wouldn't fit anywhere to the drama department. Alexa brought a new painting she'd done on a piece of tagboard—a stunning, blurry portrait of a reclining woman in blue and yellow and fuchsia—and my mom tacked it up in the living room.

"Just something to jazz up the room," Alexa explained.

Eli told jokes on the sofa. Drew brought flowers for our small table. Instant home. Despite being mad at my mom, I actually had fun. And for a few hours, I stopped thinking about my father.

On Sunday, though, when I studied while avoiding my mother's sugary attempts to kiss up to me, I wondered how long it would be before he found us in Andreas Bay and Mom moved us again.

In ten minutes, I take my last final of the semester—health. The teacher is disgustingly easy. He's just happy that about five of us in the class actually have brain cells. He gave us the final ahead of time, so those of us who "care enough," as he always says, will have no trouble. I'm not worried.

Eli sits up suddenly, "Oh my god, did you hear?"

The stage quiets. Alexa prompts him. "Hear what?" Sometimes, Eli gets drawn into his own dramatic pauses. We wait for his next comic attempt.

Instead of a joke, he tells us, "Cass Gordon's mom is in town. The cops are looking for her."

My face goes hot. "What?"

Eli nods. "The FBI's here."

Tala frowns. "How do you even know that?"

"Two of the officers were at the restaurant last night talking about it. You know Bo Perkins's dad?"

Tala rolls her eyes. "Yeah." Bo Perkins is a linebacker on the football team. Dumb as a stump, as Drew likes to say.

"He was talking with another cop, and one of the waiters overheard them."

"What did they say?" I ask, trying to appear interested but not too interested.

"They know she's here in Andreas Bay...They just don't know where yet."

Drew whistles. "They've been looking for her forever. She, like, robbed a bank or something."

"She didn't rob a bank," Alexa says. "She blew a bunch of people up. Because they were ruining the environment."

"That's not what happened," Drew argues.

"I don't know, you guys," Tala says, her brow furrowing. "It seems weird that they would be talking about it in public. I don't even think we should be talking about it."

"Well," Drew shrugs. "Bo's dumb as a stump. It's probably genetic."

"Genetics or not, it's true," Eli says. "Our own version of *The Fugitive*."

I start collecting my things. "That's intense." I try to make my tone sound off-handed. "Okay, well, I'm going to go."

Alexa looks at her watch. "Break's not over for five minutes."

"Yeah." I sling my bag over my shoulder. "I just want to do some last-minute cramming."

"Okay." She looks doubtful.

I push through the smoked-glass doors into the gray day. On the bench around the corner, I scribble a hasty note to Sam about Cass. Knowing he has his PE final this period, I wait for him by the boys' locker room. When he finally shows, thankfully alone but well after the first bell, I give him the note.

"What's this?" He looks worried.

"It's Cass," I tell him. "Read it."

I leave him unfolding the note as I hurry to beat the final bell.

• • •

I watch the evening news and scan the paper, looking for any signs that the FBI found Cass's mom.

Nothing.

Either Sam must think I'm a total idiot, or Cass was able to tell her mom to get out of town. Either way, I did something stupid or illegal. I'm hoping for illegal.

• • •

My brief brush with crime fades quickly. The four-day weekend semester break is uneventful—no police breaking down the door, brandishing the hastily written note as evidence. No whispering phone calls from Cass or Sam. Nothing. Just a call from Drew to go see the new fantasy movie playing downtown. Like the rest of the weekend, the movie—all flash and loud music and no plot—disappoints me.

I spend most of the weekend sleeping or listening to music or talking to Alexa on the phone. I fill pages in my song journal. Soon I'll need a new one. The sameness of my world is strange to me. It lulls me into a haze, and I move about like a zombie.

My mom loves her job too much to notice my funk. We don't talk about our fight, so I'm sure she thinks I've forgotten about it. I haven't. Each day, I check the answering machine and the mail. I do more Web searches. Which day will my father find me?

She comes home Monday night from her shift pink-cheeked and babbling to me about Dave, a contractor she met at the store.

"He thought he was buying cilantro, but he bought parsley instead," she tells me. "Made the salsa taste terrible. Isn't that funny?" She strips out of her jacket and hangs it on a peg by the door.

I close the book I was reading. I have been sitting on the couch so long that I imagine my body has been fused to it, my limbs blending with the fibers. "That is funny," I say, not very convincingly.

"What's wrong?" She sits down on the couch next to me, still wearing her green apron from the store, "Bay View Foods" in red script across the front.

"Nothing."

"You're still mad at me about your father."

"Just tired from finals."

"You've been moping around for days."

I motion toward the book. "Seriously, I'm just worried about school."

"You always get A's," she tells me, rubbing my knee. "Since you were tiny."

I shrug. "High school's harder."

"Not just the classes, huh?" My mother has a way of looking at me sometimes where I swear she sees all the way inside.

"I guess." I shrug again.

"Boys?" she asks.

"A boy."

She nods. "You'll tell me when you're ready to start having sex. We agreed, right?"

"Ugh, Mom." I reopen my book and pretend to read. My mother had the sex talk with me in fifth grade when I still thought boys were Martians with sweat-gland problems.

She doesn't take the hint. "Well, I want you to be safe. Not talking about it doesn't mean it won't happen." My mom's mom died when she was three, and her father never talked with her about sex. As a result, I get talked to about it far too often.

"Well, don't worry," I say. "He has to at least talk to me before there's sex."

She raises her eyebrows. "Well, let's hope so." Getting up, she pats my leg. "I got chicken for dinner. Already roasted from the deli, so I'll just make us a salad and some rice, okay? Dave says these are the best chickens in town."

"Mom?"

"Yeah?" She's already unloading the bag she brought home. I notice the tall box of Golden Grahams she sets on the counter. The kitchen, a "kitchenette" it's called, is really part of the living room, but she still has her back to me.

"Why did Rob call?"

"Rob called again?"

"No. The last time. I mean, why the warning? What did my father do that is so bad?"

She uncorks a bottle of white wine and slowly pours herself a glass. She takes a sip, purses her lips, and then looks at me. "Your father did some things…some bad things, Calle. Things that normal people don't do."

"Why was he in jail?"

Her eyebrows shoot up. "How do you know that?"

Flushing, I look at my hands folded limply in my lap. "Umm, I...I found the newspaper clipping," I whisper.

My mom plunks her glass down. "I don't think I like this habit you're making of going through my things, young lady."

Young lady? I've never gotten a "young lady" before. The skin on the back of my neck tingles. "Well, maybe if you actually told me the truth I wouldn't be forced to go looking for it in your drawers."

She shakes her head. "Oh, no. No way. You're not going to do that. You have no right to go into my drawers or anywhere else that's mine. I don't care what your reasons are."

"You don't think wanting to know my father is a good reason?" I try unsuccessfully not to raise my voice.

"I think that I've asked you to trust me about your father, to believe that I want what's best for you, and clearly, you can't do that." She turns to the bags of groceries and begins yanking food from them.

"I do believe you want what's best for me, but I don't think you necessarily know what that is." I stop, frowning. "Or that you think you do, but I don't think you do."

"That doesn't make any sense," she says.

"You know what I mean!"

She folds the empty brown bags in half and stuffs them under the sink. "I didn't want you to have to know what kind of man your father is. I was protecting you."

"What kind of man is he, Mom? Why was he in jail? Who did he assault?"

She turns, combing the hair out of her eyes with her fingers. "That time, he almost killed a man outside a restaurant. A waiter. They fought over the tip, if you can believe it. The waiter followed him outside to ask why he didn't tip him, and your father flipped out and almost killed him. Hit his head into the cement until he passed out. That's the kind of man your father is."

I can see her shaking, tears forming behind her lashes. "I was two months pregnant with you, and I watched the whole thing. All I could think the whole time he was in jail that time and after he got out and begged to come back to us, even when I let him come back, all I could think was…What if he ever turned that on you?"

Before I can say anything, she grabs her coat. "I'm going for a walk."

The door slams behind her.

I catch my mom staring at a picture of herself with Ted Number 2, both tan, both in Hawaiian-print bathing suits, margarita glasses toasting the camera. It was taken at a party two weeks before he ran off to Hawaii. I remember them posing for it, Bare Naked Ladies blaring from the speakers, my mom's head bobbing in time to the music. Ted mostly watched a girl in a white bikini all night. Sensing me behind her, my mom tucks the picture under the sofa cushions...

"HERE'S YOUR HOT COCOA." THE twenty-something girl in a Felix the Cat T-shirt sets down a steaming mug on the table next to me. I turn it so the logo of Insomnia, my favorite café, is facing toward me.

"Thanks," I say, breathing in the faint scent of cinnamon. I want to shed my day into the coffee-infused threads of the stuffed chair I'm sitting in. This morning my mom wouldn't talk to me, and at school Sam was suddenly ignoring me again. Good times.

I pull out my book. We're just starting *Friday Night Lights* in English, and I've never read it.

"Getting in some quiet reading time?" I look up at Mr. Ericson, who is standing in front of me with a to-go cup of coffee.

I smile. He looks at home here, the *New York Times* tucked under his arm, the REI jacket over his slacks and shirt, the steaming coffee in hand. "I've never read this one," I tell him.

"You'll like it, I think. It's nonfiction, which we haven't done yet this year."

I nod, study the cover of the book. Sometimes it's weird to see teachers out of school, even Mr. Ericson. Like he might grade my beverage selection or something.

He takes a breath and looks around. Sips his coffee. "Have you found anything yet? About your dad?" He lowers his voice a little, and the concerned look is back on his face. I don't want him to worry about me, but it's kind of nice that he does.

"Nothing yet," I say. "But my mom and I are talking more." That's not a total lie.

"That's great, Calle. You know, these things take time." He smiles. "Well, I'll let you get back to your reading. Enjoy."

"Thanks." I watch him push through the doors and out onto the street. The wind catches his hair and ruffles it, and he hurries a little. He's cute. In a booky, English-teacher sort of way. He passes by the window, sees me watching, and gives a little nod with his paper cup. I wave.

These things take time.

I pull my headphones back on, Zooey Deschanel's soft voice in my ears. Sighing, I return to my book. I don't really want to think about my mom or my dad or Sam or Mr. Ericson or anything at all. I just want to sit here and read.

Mom works until close tonight, so I'm on my own for dinner. Tryouts for the spring play aren't until next week, and the teachers haven't given us a lot to do. They're probably still grading our finals. I sip my cocoa and open my book.

A few pages in, I'm aware of someone staring at me through the glass of the coffeehouse window. I peek up from my book. A man. Dark, shaggy hair, a worn raincoat. My stomach flutters. Something about the angle of his shoulders holds my attention. Framed in the O of Insomnia's, he shifts slightly and his face falls out of shadow.

Jake Winter. He's just missing the pea coat. I guess sometimes things don't take as much time as you'd think.

When he sees me see him, he bolts. Tossing the book in the chair, I race outside. I look both ways. No one. Was I imagining things? Hearing my heart in my ears, I take a left around the corner just in time to see a flash of raincoat disappear down a side street.

I follow it.

"Dad?" I try, and it sounds all wrong in my mouth. "Jake Winter!" He stops and slowly turns around.

We study each other for a minute. We are only steps from each other, but we could probably jam the Grand Canyon in between us. He is much older than his picture, graying at the temples, deep lines around his eyes, but he has the same broad shoulders, the same line to his jaw.

"Hey, kid." His voice shakes a bit. I notice a gray stubble of beard on his jaw. It makes him seem older than I know he is— thirty-nine. I figured out that much from the newspaper article. He tries a smile. "I, uh…I didn't mean to sneak up on you like that. Did I scare you?"

I shake my head. My voice, it seems, has been left somewhere behind me.

"I didn't mean to if I did."

I drink in the timbre of his voice, low and strange. The faint, almost sweet smell of garbage next to the side door of a shop drifts across us, and I don't know if it is this smell that nauseates me or the sound of his voice for the first time. Its softness.

"You're so big," he says.

I flush, thinking he must mean my big bones, my baggy sweat-shirt. "It's your genes," I say, more sharply than I intend to.

He looks flustered, realizes his mistake. "No…not that kind of big. I mean, you just look so grown up. You're fifteen now, right?"

"Yes."

"And pretty. I have a pretty daughter." He smiles again. "Which doesn't surprise me at all. I can see your mom in you."

Sadness creeps across his face, and something else. Maybe regret?

"I have some of you," I say.

He seems happy about this. "My eyes," he nods.

What next to say? I bite my lip. "Where are you staying?"

"A motel out by the ocean," he says, his hands stuffing the pockets of his raincoat. "It's a cool place you got here. Remote." His eyes darken. "Hard to find."

SONGS FOR A TEENAGE NOMAD

"How did you find us?" My online searches had turned up nothing on him. And I knew his last name. Maybe I just suck at online searches.

He shrugs. "It's lucky really. A funny story. I met a guy in a bar in San Diego. He knew your mom's new guy—what's his name. Rob? So this guy was looking through a bunch of pictures his girlfriend had taken at a party. His girlfriend had just gotten them developed and wanted him to see them. One of the pictures was of Rob and his new wife. You can imagine my surprise when I recognized her. I pieced it together from there. I've gotten good at finding you guys—just my timing needs work."

Rob's phone call comes back to me. He always finds us. "We move a lot."

He raises his eyebrows. "I know."

I'm cold, having left my jacket inside on the chair. Inside with my book, with my hot chocolate, cold by now—inside with my life before. Now I am cold. And I have a father.

"Mom doesn't think I should see you."

He nods. "I know," he says again. "She..." he pauses, his eyes drifting past me, somewhere over my head. "She doesn't trust me."

"Why not?"

"Listen, Calle." He stops. "Wow, that's the first time I've said your name to you in almost fifteen years. Calle." He takes this in, this name he gave me.

"I'm listening," I say.

"I'm a good guy. I am. Your mom and I just didn't...I don't really know how to explain it." He shrugs.

"Try."

My assertiveness startles him; and then he laughs. I like its sound. "Well, you got the frankness gene from me, that's for sure."

"So I've been told."

His smile fades. "She talks about me to you?"

My turn to shrug. "Sometimes. When I ask her."

"Don't believe everything you hear," he says. "Your mom didn't leave liking me too much."

"Obviously."

"You ever listen to Paul Simon? He wrote a song once that said 'people only hear what they hear'—you ever listen to that song? Paul Simon?"

I love Paul Simon, but to him I say, "Never heard of him." That was lame, that lie. But he can't just show up in an alley and say "Paul Simon" and we're instant family. He can't do that. Besides, he totally mangled the lyric. That is not what that song says.

He shrugs as if he knows I'm lying to him. "Anyway, great song-writer. I'm a lyrics guy. You like music?"

"Sure." I think about my song journal inside in my bag in the coffeehouse, the warm coffeehouse.

"You get that from me too."

"Mom likes music," I argue. "A lot of people like music."

"Yeah, but with me, it's in my blood. I can't live without it. I think you're probably like that too." His words seem rushed, like he's trying too hard to connect us.

I rub my arms against the cold. "It's cold."

He takes a small step toward me. "We could go inside, get some coffee. We could talk."

Here it is. An invitation. A cup of coffee with my father in a nice warm coffeehouse. Not here in this cold alley like some sort of drug deal. I could ask him about the jail stuff, about his music, about when he was with my mom. We could talk.

But I say, "I kind of have a lot of homework to do."

He looks hurt, his eyes dimming. "Yeah, no...I kind of caught you off guard. I really didn't want to do that."

I don't want to chase him away, but I don't want him any closer. We just stand here between garbage cans. Water drips somewhere, a hollow, vacant sound. I have no idea what to say to him.

He says, "Maybe we could hang out sometime. I'm here. You're here. We don't have to rush anything."

It is exactly the right thing to say.

• • •

A week later, my father has not contacted me again. Maybe I shouldn't have walked away from him at the coffeehouse and left him in that alley. Should I try to call him? Should I wait? Three times, I pull the phone book out and flip through the list of motels that are near the beach: Cove Suites, the Tide Pool Inn, the Sandpiper Motel. But I don't call any of them. He can reach me. He worked this hard to find me; he won't just go away. Will he?

Friday, I come home from tryouts to find my mother cooking in the kitchenette. She's wearing an old yellow apron over slacks and a silk turtleneck sweater. Not her work clothes.

"Hey, Mom," I say, dropping my backpack by the front door. "What's up?"

"Dinner," she says brightly. "I thought we'd eat on the early side, if that's okay with you."

It's five-fifteen, and we normally don't eat until seven. She has a date. This is date behavior.

"Enjoy!" She whips off the apron and sets out two plates of food. I look at the meal: ham slices, mashed potatoes, peas. I'm not even hungry yet. Alexa, Drew, and I just ate a whole bag of chips after his audition, which apparently did not go well.

I sit down. "What's going on?"

She eats a forkful of mashed potatoes, which is about all she actually has on her plate. That and a tiny piece of ham. "What do you mean?"

I motion to the food with my fork. "Why are we having an early-bird special?"

She takes a small bite of ham slathered in yellow mustard. "Well, actually," she says. "I have a date tonight with Dave."

I nod, chewing the salty meat slowly. "Okay."

"We're going to a movie and then for a moonlight walk."

"It's freezing cold outside," I tell her. My mother still forgets that we don't live in San Diego anymore.

"I'll take a jacket." She finishes her food quickly and starts to clear her plate. Pausing, she looks down at me. I'm not even close to being done. "Oh, you're not finished." She frowns.

"I think I'll just heat this up later in the microwave," I tell her. "I'm not hungry yet anyway, and I've got some homework that I want to finish."

She beams. "Excellent!" She takes my plate into the kitchen and covers it with plastic wrap.

I flop on my bed and pull out my math. Might as well get it out of the way.

My mother comes to the doorway. She's wearing the long crimson coat we found at a thrift store in Bakersfield for five dollars. "I'm going."

"Mom?"

"Yeah?"

"Did you love my father?"

She leans her head against the doorframe. "Are we still talking about this?"

"Yes." I close my math book.

She checks her watch and frowns at me. Sighing, she comes into the room and sits on the side of the bed. "Well, he was very compelling." I nod, not understanding. Seeing my confusion, she says, "You know that bracelet I bought in Sedona?"

I can't help but laugh. "The turquoise bracelet? How can I forget it?"

My mother had seen this ridiculous bracelet at one of the small boutiques in Sedona. It was chunky and gold linked and not at all like her. Still, she'd spent half her week's paycheck on it. She wore it once, and now it sits at the bottom of her jewelry box.

"Jake was a bit like that bracelet. Beautiful at first. But not at all practical to wear."

I shake my head, smiling. "Mom, I never thought that bracelet was beautiful."

She laughs. "Well, you see through people better than I do."

She kisses my head. "Thank God." Standing, she takes another deep breath. "I'm sorry I don't talk about him with you, sweetie. I guess…" Her smile fades. "He's really painful for me to think about. Can you understand that? He hurt me. He really hurt me. It's just not something I want to talk about, and I hope you can accept that."

Shrugging, I smile up at her. "I guess I can." Now that my father has found me, I don't really need her to talk about him. He's here.

"Thank you."

"Have a good date." I cross my fingers for her. "Wait, Mom!" I call as she's leaving.

"Yeah?'

"What kind of car does he drive?"

"Dave?" she asks.

"Yeah."

"A Toyota truck," she says, raising her eyebrows.

"Not a Ford?" I smile, and she knows I'm teasing her. Her smile returns.

"No," she laughs. "Not a Ford."

• • •

A pebble hits my window.

Setting down my math book, I go to the window and peer down into the darkness. My father stands in the shadow of an old oak tree. I push open the window.

"What are you doing?" I ask him.

"I didn't want to come to the door," he whispers, hoarse.

"Why not?"

He shrugs. "Are you busy?"

"I'm doing my homework."

"On a Friday?" He laughs. "Are you sure you're my kid?"

"That's still up for debate."

Frowning, he clutches his heart. "That hurts, kid. Come on down here. Let's go do something."

I hesitate.

"Come on…" He takes a step out of shadow and looks up. "I just want to talk. Give me a chance to defend myself."

I sigh and close the window.

. . .

Thirty minutes later, I'm clutching a putter in my hand, trying to hit a golf ball through a clown mouth. My father watches me, and I pretend to concentrate on my shot. For the last three holes, we talked mostly about my grades (he can't believe I get straight A's), the drama stuff I do (I get that artist side from him, he says), and music (he can't get enough of The Who).

Now, it seems, we've run out of things to say to each other. And it only took thirty minutes. I glance over at him. He wears a black wool coat and looks like he got a haircut. He seems different than he did at the coffeehouse. Like someone gave him a full-body shoe-shine. I can see what my mom meant when she said "compelling." He's handsome. Even for a dad.

Around me, the miniature golf course is almost deserted. Apparently, the only people stupid enough to play miniature golf in the freezing wind coming off the nearby water are the two of us and a young couple who seem to be making out more than they are playing golf.

My ball goes nowhere near the clown's mouth.

"Tough shot," my father says, marking our score sheet with the stub of a pencil. He had hit it in on the first try.

I wrinkle my nose, frustrated. My hands are freezing. I retrieve my ball and try again with a little more force than I intended. The blue ball bounces off the rim of the mouth and ricochets at an angle, ending up near the hole at the next station.

"How about we just play from there?" I ask, annoyed.

My father frowns. "Aren't you having fun?"

I blow some hair from my eyes. "Oh, sure. I love not being able to feel my hands. And I'm oh so skilled at golfing."

He sighs, collecting the score sheet and his putter. "You want to get a slice of pizza or something?"

I nod. We return our putters and balls to the man at the little window where we picked them up. He reads a *Popular Mechanics*, ignoring us. Inside, the arcade is a bit more lively: kids play Skee-Ball, air hockey, and a variety of games where people kill each other. The air smells thickly of grease and ice cream. The dinner Mom made me is still sitting covered in our refrigerator. She's probably on her moonlight walk by now. I should get home soon.

I slide into an empty booth near the back.

"You like pepperoni?" my father asks, depositing his jacket on his side of the booth. I nod. Soon he returns with two huge slices of pizza. "The chick at the counter is bringing our Cokes," he tells me.

"Thanks," I say, rubbing my hands together to regain feeling.

"Sorry about the Arctic golf. I just thought..." He shrugs. "Well, I guess I just thought that's something dads and daughters do."

"Here are your drinks." A bleached blond with a belly-button ring sets down our sodas. She grins widely at Jake.

"Thanks, doll," he says, returning the smile for a bit longer than is really necessary.

I roll my eyes. "Ugh, she's, like, half your age," I say, when she is safely back behind the food counter.

"She's cute," he says, still watching her.

I take a bite of pizza and watch Bleached Blond talk to the other guy working behind the counter. He's in my Spanish class—Thad something. Looking back at my dad, I say, "All babies are cute."

He laughs. "You're really funny, you know that? You've got a good sense of humor."

I tear the paper from the straw. "What I lack in looks, I make up for in personality." I give him a wry smile.

He frowns. "What are you talking about? You're gorgeous."

"Okay," I say, pulling the last napkin out of the container. "Right."

"No, seriously." He leans forward. "You're not flashy pretty or anything. No one's going to stop and gawk on the street or anything."

"Thanks." I can feel my face reddening. Why are we still talking about this?

"But you're classic pretty," he continues. "Your type of pretty lasts forever." He leans back and picks up his slice of pizza.

I study him. "Thanks," I say again, serious now. It's a lot like what Sam said to me that day on the beach. Too bad my type of pretty means nothing in high school.

"So, Calle," he says, setting his pizza down and frowning at the empty napkin container. I offer him my crumpled napkin. Wiping his mouth, he continues, "I wanted to talk to you about something." He folds the napkin into smaller and smaller squares, his eyes cast down. "I have to leave town for a few days."

What is he talking about? He just got to town. "Why?"

"I have some business I have to take care of over in San Francisco. There's this band I'm representing now, and they have an important meeting with some A&R guy who saw their last gig. It could be big."

"Okay," I say, not sure what an A&R guy is but not wanting him to think I'm stupid.

"Hey, man," he grabs Thad-something as he walks by. Waggling the empty napkin container, my dad says, "More napkins?"

Thad grabs one off another table and clunks it down in front of us. He doesn't recognize me.

My father says, "I need you to not tell your mom about us, okay?" He drums his fingers on the table. "I don't know how she'll react. She might take off again. I just need another week."

"Another week for what?" I ask.

He fidgets in his seat and picks the pepperonis off the top of his pizza, stacking them in a little pile on the table. He has only eaten one bite from his slice; mine's almost half gone. "To get some money stuff together. Just a week. Maybe two. Then you and I can hang out. Make up for lost time. Sound good?"

The arcade lights are hurting my eyes, the noise of the place stuffing my ears with bells and sirens. He's leaving.

"Sure. Good," I say, and push the rest of the pizza away from me. Someone has just switched the music in the arcade from techno

SONGS FOR A TEENAGE NOMAD

to Bare Naked Ladies. Tonight I'll write in my journal about my father's face across the table and his smile at the blond girl, about his announcement that he will once again be exiting my life. Only this time, I'll remember him going.

CHAPTER 22
STRANGE CURRENCIES

...Red Mustang Ted listens to R.E.M. and smokes a cigarette that he tells me is very bad for me. My mother is asleep on the couch, her head in his lap. After lighting another, he asks me if I like the R.E.M. album he's playing. I play with a stuffed Pluto from Disneyland and nod, the music a swarm of bees in my ears...

"WHAT ARE YOU LOOKING AT?" I ask, dropping my backpack.

Alexa and Drew leap in front of the computer screen. "Nothing," they say in unison.

I look around the almost empty library. "Sly, you guys. Never work for the CIA. What's going on?"

Alexa shrugs and cinches her body closer to Drew. "I thought you were going to the theater."

"It's locked," I say, trying to see around them. "What are you guys looking at?"

Drew sighs. "It's just some stupid site. I'm sorry, Calle."

"Why are you sorry?" The last word catches in my throat as they pull apart like a curtain.

On the screen is a picture. Of me. In my bra and underwear. Sitting on a bench in the locker room. It is not a flattering picture. The caption reads, "Maybe they should discuss lowkarb diets in Frosh PE?"

My legs don't support me, and suddenly Drew is helping me into a chair. I can't take my eyes off the screen. "Who…" I start. But I know who. Amber's made no secret of the "amazing" camera on her iPhone.

"Hag," Alexa growls when I tell her. "I'll cram it up her prissy, rich ass!"

Drew closes the page and flips the computer screen off.

"How'd you find it?" I look up at him.

"It's Blair Stevenson's MySpace page. Where she posts stuff about school. Usually it's just complaints about teachers, boring gossip, that kind of stuff. She used to write the gossip column for the school before Ms. Jones kicked her off for being too sexual."

"And too stupid," Alexa says. "Doesn't she know 'low carb' isn't one word?"

Drew frowns at the page. "And not spelled with a 'k'? Still, she never wrote anything this mean. I was only looking at it because she does movie reviews."

"I don't even know Blair." I have one class with her. Spanish. She sits in back and writes notes all period. Everything about her looks like an overexposed picture: a little too bleached, a little too bright. She spends most of her time with her basketball-playing boyfriend. I never see her with Amber.

"Will a lot of people see this?" I look at Alexa and Drew.

They don't look back.

. . .

The note hits me in the back of my calf, and I jump. The classroom is in a test-induced hush, pencils furiously scribbling. I look around. No sign of who passed it. I see my name on the folded note, so I reach down and curl it into my palm, my eyes on Mrs. Bloom's gray head as it bends over the tests from her last class. I peek through my fingers; the handwriting is unfamiliar. I'm scared to open it. Since my PE picture posted, I've been getting all sorts of weird notes. And too many stares.

"Calle?" Mrs. Bloom is staring at me from her desk, her large fawn-colored eyes a touch suspicious. "Is there a problem?"

"No, no," I say, as thirty-two other sets of eyes swing toward me. "Just thinking."

Nodding, Mrs. Bloom goes back to her grading. The other eyes go back to their tests. Heart pounding, I quickly jam the note into the front of my binder and return to the last three problems, but they swim in front of me. I'm pretty sure I get them wrong.

Outside, I read the note. It has nothing to do with the picture. It's another poem. No one ever just writes me a "Hi, how are you?" note. No. I get riddles.

Only this one's a song. I'm sure of that, even if I don't recognize it.

> I know that you are drifting, girl,
> And look, I'm drifting too.
> Only you don't know I'm feeling

Like I can't live without you.
How can I find the words for this?
How can I describe it?
That our connection is electrical
Even as I try to hide it.
At night, the shadows wrap me up;
They bathe me in my pain.
But in the light, I'm crazy, girl,
I stumble, and I'm strange.
I know my heart's afraid of you
And know that you can't stay,
But in everything you leave here, girl,
I can only hope and pray
That you'll
Forgive me.
Forgive me.

I read the song four times, but I can't place it. Not the song. Not the band. Not the person who wrote it.

I can only guess.

Who it probably is.

And who I wish it was.

. . .

"I didn't write this," Eli says, handing the song back. "It's not even very good."

"Are you sure, Eli?" I plead. I have him cornered outside his English class. "Because it seems like something you'd do."

"Write a rockin' song to a girl I love, sure." He brushes some inky hair from his eyes. "But this," he hands the song back as if it's starting to mold in his fingers, "isn't me, and Alexa and I have been together for three weeks. Where have you been?"

He and Alexa are together? I hadn't even noticed, and I hang out with them all the time. Where *have* I been?

"Besides, I wouldn't write this kind of whiny ballad because I'm not a twelve-year-old girl," he says.

Sighing, I refold the note and put it in my pocket. "Okay, whatever."

His face softens. "I don't even recognize the handwriting."

My heart starts to hammer again. "Okay, sorry," I whisper.

"Cal, do you want me to ask around?" Eli looks worried now.

"No," I say quickly. "No. I think I know who it is. Someone's messing with me."

"Does it have something to do with the picture?"

I flush. "I don't know."

"What are you going to do about that?"

"Well, I've been really busy with all the Victoria's Secret calls I've been getting to appear in their catalog so I haven't really had time to hash out a game plan."

Eli hugs me, and I wonder why I couldn't have just loved him. Then he and I could have been together now, and everything would be so much easier.

• • •

That night I have the dream again.

Only it's not really my dream. It's the song, low and twisting through my mind, but it's unlike any dream I've had before. This time my father stands in a shadowy corner, holding a guitar. He doesn't play it, but somehow, the song comes from it, out of the little hole in the middle that the strings cross over. I can almost see the notes unfolding in the still air of the strange room.

"Hey, Mr. Tambourine Man, play a song for me..."

And my father doesn't say anything. He just smiles and holds the guitar.

...I lie flat on my back on the floor listening to Radiohead's strange, haunting music vibrate the walls of the motel room. My mom is across the street getting burritos. I know it doesn't take this long to get Taco Bell, and I imagine her in the parking lot, calling Ted Number 2 over and over on his cell phone. As the waves of Thom Yorke's voice wash through me, I wonder if Ted Number 2 even took his cell phone to Hawaii...

GAVEN LIP-SYNCS A SUPREMES SONG, waggling a long finger at us from the edge of the stage. Drew doubles over with laughter in the front row of seats, not at the song but at Gaven. From under the bouncing curls of a blond wig, Gaven shimmies back and forth in a full-length sequined gown and heels. Next to him, two other senior boys wiggle in their own sequined dresses and curly wigs. They're the opening act for the variety show to raise money for the drama classes.

"Hey, Calle, pass me that wide paintbrush." Alexa points to a pile of brushes next to the stage. I toss her the brush and finish rolling out the stretch of canvas we're cutting. The show is tomorrow night, and we're trying to get the set together. Alexa and I agreed to come in and paint some flats black and hang a large canvas cutout of a comedy-drama mask. We thought it would only take a couple of hours, but we've already been here two hours, and we're not even halfway done. A half hour ago, we sent Eli out for food.

Gaven and his "girls" finish their song; Drew applauds wildly. When Gaven notices Sara in the back of the theater, he shouts, "Hey, Sara! I'm hot, don't you think? Kind of makes you wish you didn't turn me down for Homecoming this year."

Sara takes in his wig, his dress, and his shoes. Wryly, she says, "I'm quite sure Diana Ross did not wear a blond wig." Turning her back on him, she returns to her conversation with Tala.

Gaven clutches his heart. "Ouch. She kills me," he smiles. His gesture flashes me to the image of my father, standing below my window and clutching his own heart.

"Hey, you okay?" Alexa pauses with her paintbrush.

I stay focused on the canvas. "Sure, why?"

"You just got a really weird look on your face for a minute."

"I just got a whiff of that paint. How can you stand it?"

Smiling, she returns to the flat. "It's not so bad."

"Hey, you guys," Sara calls to us. "Tala and I are going to get food. Do you want anything?"

Alexa shakes her head. "We sent Eli already."

Sara smiles. "Make sure you get your change back." Laughing, she and Tala leave through the glass doors.

"Hey," I say to Alexa. She looks up at me, hand poised over a flat. "I'm happy for you and Eli. Sorry I've been kind of out of it and didn't say anything."

She flushes. "Thanks. I thought maybe…I thought maybe you were mad about it."

"No! Not at all. I'm really happy for you guys."

She looks at me, eyes wide, and then giggles. I have never heard Alexa giggle like that before. She says, "I'm really happy too. He's… he's great." Just talking about him makes her glow.

I nod, something tightening in my chest. "He is great."

We get back to work.

Drew hops up on stage and speaks into the microphone. "Testing, one, two…" He's MC for the show tomorrow, so he needs to practice his opening stand-up routine. Now that Gaven is done, Drew has the stage to himself. Lucky us.

Maybe he thinks if he kisses up enough to Ms. Hecca, she'll forgive his lousy audition and cast him anyway. We'll see; she posts the cast list for the spring play on Monday. No one's very excited. This year Hecca decided to do Shakespeare instead of student-written pieces.

"Should I cut this out?" I ask Alexa, who has dragged the ladder onstage to work on the doorframe.

From the ladder she looks down and nods. "Did Hecca say she wanted a curtain on this doorway?" she asks me.

"Yeah. Or a back flat." I move to the front of the stage and start cutting carefully around the mask Alexa drew for me on the canvas at lunch today.

"Curtain's easier," she mumbles, climbing down off the ladder.

The door pushes open, letting in a cold whoosh of early February air. Thinking it's Eli with the food, we all turn, but it's Sam, blinking away the daylight. He spots me, slides his hands into his pockets, and says, "Hi." He looks nervously at Alexa and Drew.

Alexa freezes on the stage and looks at Drew quickly, then at me. Drew just raises his eyebrows and goes back to checking the microphone, tapping it with his finger. Thump, thump, thump.

"Hi," I say back, still crouched over the half-cut mask.

"Umm…" Sam licks his lips. "Can I talk to you for a second?" He pauses, then adds, "Alone."

I set down the scissors and stand up. "Sure." Seeing him there, standing red-cheeked from the cold, I suddenly can't breathe.

Alexa walks downstage and stands next to me, placing her hand on my arm. "What's this all about, Sam?" she asks.

"It's no big deal," I whisper, my face burning.

"No, it is a big deal," she tells me. "Some of us are tired of him jerking you around."

"Alexa, I…" Sam starts.

"I'm not talking to you," she snaps. She tucks her red curls behind her ears and looks at me. "You've been sulking around for two months. Don't tell me he has nothing to do with it."

I don't tell her that. I don't tell her that it's Sam and so much more.

"You're not at his beck and call, Calle," Drew says into the microphone. It echoes off the walls. Sam jumps a little. Drew lowers the mike and stares hard at him.

"I'll just go," Sam says.

"No, wait!" I look at Alexa, and say, "I'm fine."

She looks worried but returns to the ladder, casting a suspicious glance at Sam. I know she's just trying to protect me; it's sweet of her, but I want to see what carried him in here after weeks of ignoring me.

I walk down the aisle and take his arm, feeling their eyes on us.

"Come on," I say. "Let's talk outside."

Outside the light is strong and clear. Cold winter light and a thick blue sky. I shiver a bit at the temperature change and hope my nose doesn't start running.

Trying to smile, Sam says, "Your friends don't like me."

I make sure I don't smile even as my heart does little flips at his attempt. "Have you given them reason to?" I fold my arms across my chest.

"Alexa can be a little bossy."

I shrug. "She has a point. They both have a point."

"Okay," he sighs, the smile long dead on his lips. "I'm sorry."

I wait, refusing to make this easy for him.

"I'm sorry about our situation," he says.

"What situation is that?" I try to sound casual, but my voice comes out strange, choked.

He takes his hands out of his pockets and motions to the space between us. "This," he says. "Us."

"I'm not aware there is an 'us.'"

He sighs, frustrated. "You know what I mean. You and me. That nothing…that we didn't…work out," he finishes. "I feel like you glare at me in the hallways, that you hate me."

"I don't glare at you."

"Well, it feels like you do." His eyes search my face.

I can't meet his gaze; it bores into me, so I stare at his shoes. "I have other things on my mind besides you, Sam."

"You mean your dad?"

I shrug, not trusting him with this sudden introduction of my father. I haven't told anyone about the coffeehouse, the miniature golf, the pebble at my window. "Why do you even care?"

"I care, Calle. I do. I really like you."

Anger flares through me. "Really? Because you don't seem like you like me. I don't ignore the people I like, avoid their eyes, never talk to them. If you like me, you pretty much suck at showing it. You sure didn't seem to care much when your little amateur-photographer friend decided to have a go at me!"

"I made her take it off!"

The picture had disappeared a day after it was posted. But it didn't matter. It didn't stop someone from putting a "Porn Star" sticker on my locker.

"I can't believe you would be with someone who would do that to another person."

He shakes his head as if to clear it. "I told Amber how stupid that was. She thinks she's being funny."

"She knows exactly what she's doing."

He throws up his arms in frustration. "You don't understand, okay? I'm sorry about Amber. I'm sorry she did that to you, but I can't take it away. That's not the point. I came here to tell you… it's just that…you and I…we just can't be together right now. It won't work."

"That's clear," I say, again to his shoes.

"It's not clear. Nothing's clear." There's a catch in his voice that draws my eyes to his face. To his eyes. He is crying. I take half a step back. He wipes furiously at his cheeks. "You don't understand my life right now…it's too hard."

"You don't let me understand, Sam. You don't give me a chance to."

"Calle?" Eli stands several feet away with clear plastic bags of chips and sandwiches, and a tray of sodas. He looks worriedly from me to Sam. "Are you okay?"

I shake my head but say, "I'm fine. It's fine. Thanks." Sam turns away from Eli and puts his hands back in his pockets.

Eli nods slowly. "I got you a sandwich and a root beer. When you're ready."

"Thanks," I smile at him, my heart swelling with him—his glossy hair and dark eyes. "I'll be right there."

"Okay." He darts another look at Sam. "I'll be inside if you need me."

I nod and turn back to Sam. The door to the Little Theatre opens and shuts.

"Great," Sam says. "Now he thinks I'm an idiot."

I shrug. "It's okay. He already thinks you're an idiot. He thinks all football players are idiots."

Sam's face flushes. "That's not fair…"

I interrupt, "Relax. I'm kidding."

"Oh," he mumbles.

"We don't think so badly of you," I say. I look closely at his face, the tears matting his lashes, his red-blotched cheeks. A blurred version of cute. When I cry, I look like a blowfish, all swollen and awkward.

His eyes well again. "I'm sorry," he whispers.

I pull him toward me, holding the back of his curly head with one hand, and his weight shifts down into me, the side of his face resting into my shoulder like a child's. Through the Little Theatre window, I imagine I can see all three of them—Drew, Eli, Alexa— with their noses pressed to the glass, watching us.

. . .

The next week at Burger Mania, a hand reaches for my tray of fries, and I slap it away. "Just one," Eli whines.

Laughing, I hand him the tray. "Have as many as you want. They go well with my burger you just ate."

Toby laughs and helps himself to some of my fries as well. Sara just sips her Sprite and shakes her head. "You two are such pigs. How can you eat three cheeseburgers?"

"We're growing boys," Toby says, rubbing his flat stomach.

"Yeah," Eli agrees. "Growing boys need cheeseburgers."

Alexa stirs her vanilla shake with her straw. "I don't think that's actually a rule."

"Here's Drew," Sara says, scooting over in the circular booth so Drew can slide in beside her. He slumps into the seat and buries his head in his arms.

"How'd it go?" Alexa asks.

"Terribly." His voice is muffled but weighted with despair.

"Did you tell her we can switch roles?" Toby asks, eating the rest of my fries. "I'm running track this year. I don't have time to play Lysander."

Sara looks skeptically at Toby. "You're running track?"

He shrugs. "Sure. It looks good for college."

"I hope you stopped smoking, or you won't make it once around," she says. He shows her the patch on his arm. "Well, bravo." She drains the rest of her Sprite. "Scooch out, Drew. I'm getting a refill."

He picks himself up and allows her past. "Could you get me some onion rings?" he asks, brushing at some crumbs on his "I do my own stunts" T-shirt.

"Sure."

He settles back into the booth. "She said she won't even talk to me about the audition until tomorrow. I have to think about it and write her a letter."

Eli smiles. "I had to write her a letter last year for the David Ives's tribute. Just tell her you learned a lot from not being prepared for your audition, blah, blah, blah." He motions to Sara at the counter. "More fries," he tells her. She rolls her eyes.

Drew shrugs. "She told me to read the part, that I get to play 'the Wall,' and it's really funny. Whatever."

Toby leans across the table. "Dude, you have to switch with me. I can't remember all those lines. She just gave me the part because there weren't enough guys who tried out."

"I tried out."

"Oh, right."

Drew slides over and lets Sara sit back down. He dunks a hot onion ring into some ketchup. "Yum," he says. "Thanks." Sara pats his head.

Eli looks wounded. "Where are my fries?"

"You've had enough," Sara says, her green eyes laughing.

"You're not my mom."

"No, but today I'm your bank account, so it's the same thing." She smiles at me. "Did you get enough? Eli ate practically all of your food."

"I'm fine," I say.

"So who's going to the Sweetheart Dance this Friday?" Sara asks, popping one of Drew's onion rings in her mouth.

"Not me," Toby says, chewing the ice from his soda.

"Yes, you are. Tala told me you two were going," Sara tells him.

"Oh, yeah."

Drew says, "I'm going."

"With who?" Sara asks. "You have to have a date, or they won't let you in."

Toby mutters, "Student Council date Nazis...it's so stupid. How can they even get away with that?"

Drew smiles. "I'm taking Greta, my blow-up doll. Let's see them not let me in." Toby laughs so hard he almost spits root beer across the table.

Alexa turns to Sara. "Did Gaven ask you? He couldn't shut up about it at the show last weekend."

"Yes," Sara rolls her eyes. Gaven's been madly in love with her for a year, but she always blows him off. "And to Senior Ball already. I can't wait until he graduates. No, for Sweetheart's I'm going with Kevin Timbers."

Toby makes a little "whoo, whoo" noise, and Sara swats him.

"Hey, Calle?" Eli asks. "Do you want to go with me?" The table takes an audible intake of air. Alexa's eyes widen. He says quickly, "Just friends. Alexa's going to be in the city with her parents all weekend."

"We're bonding," she says. She tries to sound light, but I can see her smile sagging at the edges. She stirs her shake.

"I don't know…" I start.

"You guys should go," she says to me. "It's fine."

"Are you sure?" I watch her closely. The rest of the table watches with me.

"Oh my god, you guys, it's fine," she says. "Someone needs to make sure he doesn't eat all the Oreos. And do not, I repeat, do not let him dance." She's laughing now. "Seriously, go."

"Okay, sure, Eli," I say. "That'd be fun."

"Okay, so let's meet before as a group and grab dinner," Sara suggests. "At seven."

"Let's meet here," Eli says. "I think I owe Calle some french fries."

"And a burger," I say.

• • •

The dance looks like Cupid threw up on it. Pink, red, and purple hearts inked with couples' names cling to the walls under fat strands of glittery silver and pink garland. Tables are covered with pink butcher paper. A giant spinning orb in the center of the ceiling spits tiny fragments of red, white, and pink light around the room.

"Gross," Drew says, pushing through the red and pink streamers in the doorway. "It's like a Hallmark card exploded." He holds Greta, the blow-up doll, tightly around her middle. She is wearing a corsage he bought her on her blow-up wrist.

Tala sighs and leans into Toby. "I think it's nice."

"Hi, guys!" Cruise Director Kayla smiles widely at us as she takes our tickets. "Happy Valentine's Day!" She is dressed head to toe in red: red jeans, red sweater, red shoes, and she has a giant white carnation affixed to her shoulder. She spots Greta. "Umm...?"

"She's with me," Drew says, and hands over her ticket.

"Umm, okay. Carnations are one dollar at the sophomore table!" she tells us, her voice high and squeaky.

"Thanks, Kayla!" Drew says overzealously.

"Cute shirt," she points at Drew's "I'm what Willis was talkin' 'bout" T-shirt. He gives her a thumbs-up. She giggles and turns toward the next group coming through the streamers. "Have fun!"

"She must run on an extra generator," Drew whispers, clearly disappointed that Greta hadn't caused more of a stir.

Tala punches him lightly on the shoulder. "She's nice."

Eli takes my hand and walks me toward the buffet table. "Look!" He points. "Oreos."

I get a cup of red punch and watch Eli and Drew eat six Oreos each. The DJ is playing old fifties love songs; "Earth Angel" drifts across the confettied light of the dance floor.

"There's a lot of people here," Tala says to me, looking at the already crammed dance floor.

I nod, sipping my punch. I watch her drag Toby onto the dance floor. They seem so happy, arms wound around each other. What must it be like to just come to a dance with your boyfriend? Both parents at home watching a movie or something? It's been three weeks, and there is no sign of my father. My mom was right. Compelling and completely unreliable. As I scan the dance floor, I try not to think about him.

Then my eyes fix on a couple locked in the almost motionless rocking rotation of a slow dance.

Drew sees them too. "Damn," he says, putting his drink down on the table. "Hey, come have an Oreo."

"It's okay," I tell him. "I see them."

He sighs. "He's an idiot."

I watch Sam hold Amber in slow revolving circles. I halfheartedly agree, "He is an idiot."

A Beyoncé song replaces "Earth Angel." I guess that's it for the fifties. The body lock on the dance floor disperses. Some couples move into the fast dance, while others drift off toward the food tables. I lose sight of Sam in the shift.

I notice Eli watching me from across the table. He wiggles his eyebrows and smiles. I try to smile back.

He tosses an Oreo on the table. "I'm a bad date," he announces. "I go straight to the cookies. I should ask if you want to dance."

"I don't want to dance," I say.

"But I," he says, grabbing both my hands and sweeping our arms out to the side, "am a marvelous dancer." He drags me out onto the floor, just at the edge near the bathrooms, and proceeds to dance around me, kicking his heels behind him and to the sides. I see Drew over by the snack table, laughing.

"What do you call that?" I ask him.

"I call it the Sweetheart Dance!" He shakes his whole body,

hooking his thumbs right and left. His red pants make swishing noises, and I notice he's tied tiny jingle bells to his shoes.

"You look like you're being electrocuted," I tell him.

The music fades from fast to soft, but he keeps dancing at the same pace as before. "You do not like my dance of love?" he croons, adopting a fake French accent.

"The music's not even fast." I can hear Drew laughing.

Eli stands up straighter, cocks his head to the side, and listens. I can't help but giggle. "You're right!" he says. "It's a slow song." Without warning, he pulls me into his arms. "We must mash ourselves together now!"

We start to dance, his hand holding mine, his arm around my back. Still giggling, I rest my head against his shoulder. His heart is banging through his shirt.

After a moment, I feel someone watching us. Looking up, I see Sam leaning against the wall by the bathroom. His arms are folded across his chest. When he sees me notice him, he strides over to us.

"What's going on?" he asks gruffly. He stands a bit too close. I can't help but back up, away from Eli, away from both of them. Eli eyes him.

"I'm dancing," I say slowly.

He nods with just a bit too much emphasis. "Oh, uh-huh?" He darts a look at Eli. "I thought you said he wasn't your boyfriend."

"He's not my boyfriend."

"I'm not her boyfriend," Eli says.

Sam runs his hand through his hair and points exaggeratedly at Eli. "You're kind of chummy with him." He gets in close to me, his breath hot on my face. "Kind of close!" He reeks of beer, which explains why he seems too elastic, his gestures too overstated. "At least I've been honest with you!" he sputters.

"Honest with me?" I repeat, stunned. "I'm sorry, when were you honest with me?"

"I explained about Amber!" He is close to shouting and has now drawn a crowd from our part of the dance floor.

I rub my temples. The DJ is playing Lady Gaga's "Bad Romance" and my head is pounding with it. "I'm leaving."

I turn to go, but Sam reaches out and grabs my arm, pulling me back. "Wait!"

"Ow!"

It doesn't really hurt; it's more of a reaction, but it's enough to make Eli grab Sam and wrench his arm from me. "Leave her alone!"

With a cry, Sam shoves Eli. They are roughly the same height, but Sam probably outweighs him by forty pounds, so Eli goes flying and ends up sprawled on the floor by the bathrooms, his hair in his face.

"Stop it!" I hear myself screaming. The room is spinning with shreds of jagged colored light. I think I might throw up. Most of the kids have stopped dancing and have formed a half-ring around us. No music now. Someone probably went to get a teacher.

In the silence, punctuated by spinning flecks of light, I look at both of them, at Eli gazing up from the floor, at Sam blinking down at him, a look of surprise on his face. Then my eyes are drawn to the figure by the bathroom door, standing immobile, a small beaded purse spinning from its satin cord clutched in her hand. Amber. Her eyes meet mine, and she turns and runs from the room.

CHAPTER 24

PART OF MY LIFE

...Sacramento sun pours through the wide windows, carrying with it a hint of late September chill. With the smell of Sunday brunch thick in the air around us—blueberry scones, a steaming ham-and-cheese quiche, the thick espresso that Dan drinks on weekends—Mom and I spin around the kitchen singing as loud as we can, India Arie pulsing through the speakers in the ceiling...

IN PE ON MONDAY, I jog over to Ms. Davis. "Can I use the bathroom, please?" She nods and motions toward the locker rooms.

Inside, the locker room is empty and smells of strawberries. Someone must have used body spray earlier; the air is thick with the chemical smell of fake fruit essences. At the sink I wash my hands and fix my ponytail. Noticing a smudge of dust on my cheek (probably from the disgusting mats they make us use), I lean into the mirror. Out of the corner of my eye, I see someone behind me.

"I want you to stay away from him," Amber says.

Turning, I see she's been crying. She holds a wadded tissue in her hand, and her eyes are red rimmed. She is not dressed for gym, so she must have been sitting in the locker room. Ms. Davis always excuses crying girls from class. Especially on rainy days.

"Maybe you should talk to *him*," I say, my hands starting to shake. "He's the one who keeps approaching me."

"Maybe you should stay away from other girls' boyfriends." Her voice would be threatening if it didn't sound so hollow in the middle, like words through a straw.

My mind flashes to the picture she posted of me, and it's all I can do not to smash her perfect, freckle-flecked nose. "Maybe you should tighten his leash. He doesn't seem to want to stick around on his own."

She takes a step closer, and I press back slightly into the sink. "You think you're so smart," she says. "But look at you." Her eyes rake over me. "You need to take another look at that picture. Because smart can't fix fat."

I swallow against the knot in my throat and lean forward until my face is inches from hers. "You know what's sad, Amber? You're as pretty as you are, and he still doesn't like you. At least I don't have to stalk him to get him to kiss me."

Her face pales. She points a long, thin finger at me. "Just stay away from him…"

She's cut off by the swing of the door. Cass enters, wearing her PE top and a pair of jeans. At the sight of Cass, Amber freezes.

Cass spots us and places her hands on her hips. "Well, well, well," she grins, her gaze slipping from Amber to me. "What's the story, ladies?"

"It's none of your business, Cass," Amber snarls. "We're just talking."

Cass sidles up and puts her face very close to Amber's. "I don't think I like your tone, Pampers."

"Don't call me that."

Cass turns to me. "You see, we call her Pampers because Amber used to wet her pants in second grade, isn't that right?" She smiles sweetly at Amber, whose face turns scarlet.

Blinking tears, Amber says, "Shut up, Cass. At least I'm not a freak!"

Cass's shove sends Amber stumbling back. Cass takes a deep breath and surveys her. "Are you going to finish what you started, or should you just leave now?" she asks, her voice low.

Amber looks at me and then at Cass.

"I hate you both!" she yells before pushing her way out through the doors. We hear her footsteps pound up the metal steps to the main part of the gym.

Cass rolls her eyes. "Yeah, it keeps me up at night." Turning to me, she sucks in her lower lip and then says, "We should go. Pampers will tattle."

She starts toward the back of the locker room.

"Where are we going?" I trail behind, adrenaline still surging through me.

"You'll see." Looking at me, she says, "You should change." She slips on a gray sweatshirt.

I hesitate.

"Oh, come on," she says, waiting.

While I quickly pull on my school clothes, she unlatches the chain around the back door and pushes it open a crack. Peering out, she says, "All clear," and disappears.

She holds the door for me. Grabbing my backpack and Walkman, I follow her outside into the thin rain.

• • •

Cass parks her truck by the old lighthouse trail.

"The lighthouse is closed on Mondays," I tell her.

"I know." She climbs out of the truck and starts walking the trail toward the beach.

The fog and rain mix in ragged swirls. Fingers of it spread across the trail, and at times I can't see Cass several yards ahead. Soon, though, we're at the base of the lighthouse, its peeling paint in reach of our hands.

Cass vanishes around the side. Alone, I stare into the shifting fog and try to locate the direction of the beach. Screeching seagulls and the thunder of the waves seem to hover all around me. The light is something otherworldly, not day, not night. I blink rain from my eyes and press my hands to my freezing cheeks. School seems an ancient land, something in a galaxy far away from this strange, floating ghost world.

"Calle!" Cass hisses through the damp. "Come here."

I walk toward her voice, and two shapes emerge from the fog. At first I think Cass is with a child, and then I realize she's found Emily, the old woman from the football game. She's even smaller than I remember and as wispy as the sea grasses. She clicks open the door to the lighthouse with a huge metal ring of keys, smiles at Cass, and motions for us to go inside.

"Thanks, Emily." Cass says.

"Thanks," I say, and I can see her face register mine.

"Calle girl. No nachos to share today?" Her laugh seems part of the air.

"I'm afraid not," I tell her.

"Well, you girls go on up." She waves at the doorway. "No sense in us getting any more soaked than we already are."

"We won't be too long," Cass says.

"You won't see a darn thing today, but that's not really the point, is it?" Her voice seems to linger as she evaporates into the fog.

We climb the circular stairs to the top. Emily is right. The world is a dense white blanket against the sweeping windows of the light-house. Cass presses her hand to the glass and seems to look through it all.

"Isn't it great up here?" she asks.

"Amazing," I say, watching the mist churn and undulate. "Like being inside a washing machine."

Cass nods, continuing to stare out into it.

I look around the circular room, all metal and glass. Incredible to think that a hundred years ago, this lonely lighthouse guided ships away from the jagged rocks offshore, that it saved the lives of equally lonely sailors.

"I'm glad you cut with me," Cass says, her breath making tiny clouds on the glass. "I didn't think you would at first. You're such a brainiac."

"I just wanted to get out of there."

She laughs. "That's how I feel every day."

"Me too."

She turns away from the glass and looks at me. "Because of Sam?"

I shrug and sit on a small wooden bench against the wall.

"He doesn't really like Amber," she says. "She's just a habit. Like biting your nails."

"I know," I say. "I just wish he didn't bite his nails in public."

She laughs. "Sam's a hard one to figure out," she says. "Not like the other boneheads he hangs with. They're transparent."

I nod, kicking at the bench with my heel.

"You're good for him, I think," she says, cocking her head and studying me.

"I'm not so sure." What I'm most unsure of is her relationship with Sam. Maybe she'll tell me. My heart flutters, and I lick my dry lips. Cass pulls her sweatshirt up to her elbows, and I notice that there's writing on her left arm, blue ink pen. It reads, "In solitude, I am actual."

"What's that quote from?" I ask, pointing. "On your arm?"

She glances down. "From second period today. Health."

I shake my head. "No, I mean, whose is it? Who wrote it"

She studies her arm. "I did. Sometimes when I'm bored in class—which is all the time—I write down things that pop into my head. I just didn't have any paper today."

"I do that too. Not on my arm. In my journal. Only they're mostly songs. Songs that make me remember."

She nods. "I've seen you writing in it at school."

"What does it mean?" I ask her.

"It means I'm my purest self only when I'm alone. And when I'm using my own words." She shrugs. "It just went through my head, that's all. And it was a hell of a lot more interesting than Mrs. Jenner droning on and on about disease prevention."

We both listen to the swish of wind outside for a while and the creak of the lighthouse, this washing machine world growing familiar around us.

Finally Cass says, "I want to tell you about my mom."

I sit up. "Okay."

She sighs, running a hand through her hair. She must have just cropped it a few days ago; it's never been this short before. Turning to me, she says, "Sam told me what you did. The note." I nod. "That was really cool."

The more I thought about that note afterward the more I believed it was a stupid thing to do. But I don't tell her this. I say, "Thanks."

"She screwed up a long time ago, you know? Ancient history." She leans back into the glass. Behind her, the mist continues to swirl, occasionally shot through with laces of light from an unseen sun. "I don't know how much you know."

I try for honesty, and the words are sticky. "I heard she's wanted by the FBI." In the hollow room, they sound like an accusation.

She nods and folds her arms across her chest. "She is. When she was young, way before I was born, she belonged to this group, this activist group in New York. They were protesting some company that was knocking down some community building. A whole bunch of people were going to end up homeless.

"Anyway, one of the guys in her group was crazy—a total nut job. And he set a small bomb at the company's headquarters. No one was supposed to be working that night. He was just trying to scare them. It was an accident," she explains, "but it still left a dead guy."

"Oh my god." Fumbling for something to do, I dig in the front pocket of my backpack for my ChapStick and smear it quickly across my lips.

She watches me, purses her lips, and breathes out slowly. "Yeah. It's pretty major. Anyway, she panicked and ran. Came out here to her brother. Had me. Then took off again. Now she's always running." She pauses and turns back to the window.

I nod, knowing something about that. "And your dad?"

She hesitates, not turning from the window. "She told me he died."

"Do you see her?" I don't know if the answer to this will push me back into the world of crime, but I ask anyway.

"Sometimes," she says. "Never for very long. This last time I only saw her for fifteen minutes. Now I won't see her for years. My uncle takes care of me. Has my whole life. But she's still, you know, my mom." She looks back at me. "I figured you'd understand, what with your dad situation and all."

"I understand." I know what it's like now to have fifteen minutes of your life mean so much.

"You and your mom still fighting about it?" she asks.

"Not really." Outside, the mist continues to form a cocoon around us. We might be the only two people in the world. "He found me," I find myself telling her.

"What?" Cass turns from the window.

"My dad," I say. "He came here. To Andreas Bay. We had pizza."

"Seriously? What was that like?"

Like talking into a dream, I tell her about the coffeehouse, the miniature golf, him leaving again. "It was so weird, like it didn't even really happen."

"What does your mom think?"

I shake my head. "She doesn't know. She'd flip if I told her, and we'd just move again. All our moves, all the new places, my whole life has been about keeping away from him." I pull my sweatshirt arms down over my cold hands. "Anyway, it doesn't matter. He said he'd be back in a week, two at the most, and it's been almost a month. I'm not holding my breath."

"Maybe he really had work to do, like he said." Cass bites her lip and looks like she doesn't really believe what she's saying. "Or maybe he just doesn't know how to be your dad, and you'll have to show him."

"Maybe." I take a deep breath, weighing her words. Maybe I have to try harder. He doesn't know how to be a father. "You know, it's hard," I say, almost to myself.

"At first, I just had all this crap at school. Sam and Amber, all that. Then I had all the stuff at home. My mom not telling me about my dad and trying to find out more about him without her knowing. Now, though, I have to make a decision—what do I want my relationship with him to be? Now, it's on me. And that's harder."

"Yeah," Cass agrees, looking back out at the swirling world. "That's way harder. So, what do you want it to be?"

"I don't know." I stare into the mist, willing it to have answers that I know aren't there.

. . .

After Cass drops me off downtown, I stand in the rain and look at the road leading to Sam's house. I think about the dance last week, about his breath in my face, about how hard he shoved Eli. I walk the mile up the hill to his house. At least I can fix one messed-up thing in my life.

As I ring the doorbell, I feel ridiculous. And wet. My hair is plastered to my head, and my thin jacket is soaked clear to my sweatshirt. I wait, the haunted doorbell echoing through halls I have never seen. I am just about to turn away when the door is pulled violently open.

Sam stands there, breathing heavily. "Oh," he says. On his head, a cut drips red blood; there are splotches of it on his pale-green shirt. Behind him, something shatters.

"They won't take me there!" a banshee voice cries from somewhere in the depths of the house. "Nooooooooo!" More glass breaking. Sam looks fearfully over his shoulder.

"Calle, this is a bad time," he says. "You've got to get out of here."

"What's going on?" I try to peer over his shoulder. A beige wall with the picture of a sailboat. A mahogany table with a vase of white roses. Withered white roses. All thoughts of the dance drain out of me. His life, at least right now, seems more messed up than mine. The house itself seems to tremble with heartache. "What happened to your head?"

He touches the cut, as if for the first time. "It's nothing. You should go."

Footsteps sound in the hallway. In seconds, a woman is at the door. She is unmistakably his mother. Her coppery curls are loose on her shoulders, matted and sticking out in various directions. Her feet are bare, and she wears a black-velour sweat suit. The top is unzipped to her waist, exposing a pale-pink lace bra and white belly. I take a step backward.

"Who are you?" she demands, tears spilling from her large eyes. "I'm not going."

"I'll just see you at school," I say to Sam, starting to back away. "Sorry."

I see her collapse into the doorframe, spilling down it like water thrown against a wall. Sam struggles to pull her inside, his frightened gaze trying to be on me and her at the same time. Then, she turns to dead weight in his arms.

I don't try to help. I don't say anything. I don't know why but I can't. It's too much. Instead, I race away down the driveway.

• • •

"Calle! Calle!"

I try to ignore the voice and keep running, but a cramp seizes my side, and I can't run anymore. Hands on my knees, I bend over and try to take in air.

"Hey," Sam is panting beside me. "Wait up, will you?"

It has stopped raining, but the misty air has turned his cut into a watery, drippy mess and expanded the bloodstains on his shirt.

I slowly catch my breath and watch him catch his.

"I'm really sorry," I start. "I don't know why I ran."

"Look," he says. "You can't say anything about what you saw, okay?" He grabs both my wrists and stares down at me.

"I don't know what I saw," I say, wrenching my hands from his grasp. "What's going on? I mean, the Valentine's dance…that," I point up to his house.

"I want to tell you," he says. "I just can't. I have to get back to her. She can be…she can hurt herself when she gets like this." I notice that he's in sock feet, and that they are soaked through and muddy. He shivers.

"You always say you can't talk about it. It's ridiculous. Why can't you just talk to me?" I am shivering too. The words stumble out.

"Calle." He holds both my shoulders. "Right now I need you to promise that you won't say anything to anyone about this. Promise me."

"Where's your dad?"

"At the store." His eyes darken. "He's not very involved right now. It's just me." He exhales and then says again, "Please promise." His voice is choked with desperation. "Please. It's a small town."

"I promise," I whisper.

"Can you meet me at the bar later? I know it's a school night, but I really want to talk to you about this."

"Give me a couple of hours. I'll be there by eight at the latest," I say with more certainty than I feel.

Nodding, he gives my shoulders a brief squeeze, then turns and runs back up the hill toward his house, his wet sock feet slapping the asphalt, leaving muddy prints that soon fade into the wet ground.

• • •

I know it's my father inside, not by his voice but by my mom's. It has an edge, like the low roil of near-boiling water. The front door hangs open a crack, and I stay right near it in the shadows and listen.

She is saying, "I don't want your life. I don't want that life for Calle."

"We can put it behind us, Alyson. All behind. We can be a family."

"I can't. You haven't changed."

My father's voice is all butter and soft syllables. "I've changed. You don't know. You never gave me a chance. I wanted her in my life, and you never gave me a chance."

My insides swim with his words. I am still digesting the scene I witnessed at Sam's, still processing it after the hour I spent walking alone downtown, and now my father is here. Talking with my mom. And he wanted me all along. All this time. I strain to hear my mother's response.

"You gave up that chance when you made your choice." Roiling water, churning and churning.

What choice? When he went to jail? I hold my breath, frustrated. It's like listening to only one side of a phone conversation; the other side is an unspoken history.

"I was trying to keep food on the table. Someone had to work, and you didn't want to." His voice loses a soft fold. I hear anger beneath it.

"I had a baby!"

"And I had to work!"

The water of Mom's voice hits boiling. "Selling drugs?" Her voice is up an octave. "Some career for a father to have. How could I keep our daughter there? How, Jake?"

My eyes widen. Drugs? He's a musician. He has a band. I lean closer, trying to look through the narrow slat of the open door, but I can't see them.

"My music was about to hit. You remember the manager from Philadelphia. We were so close. If you'd been more supportive. Who knows? I might have gone somewhere if I hadn't had to deal with you."

"It's my fault? You didn't make it because of me?" My mother sounds like she's in the kitchenette now. A drawer opens and shuts. "Maybe if you'd spent more time playing music than shooting up, the guy from Philadelphia might have had something to listen to."

"Don't act so superior. You had no problem with my career," his voice drips sarcasm, "when you were using it, did you?"

I flinch. My mom won't even eat refined sugar; there is no way she used drugs.

"I want you to get out, Jake. I want you to stop following us, stop harassing us. I'll call the police." My mother's voice is shaking.

"Call them. Tell them you kidnapped our daughter, that I've spent the last fourteen years trying to find her. Tell them that." I can hear his heavy footsteps pacing the living room. "Call them!"

"You've spent most of those last fourteen years in jail," my mother shouts back.

"You never gave her my letters, never gave me a chance. Or gave her a chance to know me. You stole her from me."

"She was a little girl. Ouch, Jake, let go…"

I push open the door. My father holds my mother's arm tight, wrenching it toward him.

"Let go," she shouts again, her hair in her face, before they both see me and freeze. A twisted tableau. It doesn't seem real. Like the game we play in drama rehearsal warm-ups where two people act a scene until an audience member shouts "Freeze!" and then steps in and changes it, using the same position to create a totally different scene.

I wish I could change this freeze. Make it a happy family. Maybe the mom and dad would be dancing. They could be ice skating or helping one another into a boat. Not hurting each other. Not shouting about drugs and kidnapping.

I find a voice I don't recognize and use it. "Let her go."

My father lets go and takes a step back. My mom pushes her hair out of her eyes.

None of us says anything for a very long time. My head throbs, and I am aware of the hum of the heater, the tick of the clock on the wall. My parents stand at strange angles before me, as if they don't know what to do with their body parts, so they just let them hang there.

Suddenly, I am filled with the song—"*Hey, Mr. Tambourine Man…*"echoes through my head. But even as it comes to me, it fades. I look at the man frozen in the middle of our small, dim living room. My Tambourine Man. My whole life, I've wanted this father. But I can't have the scene before me, not this fractured portrait. So I will write my own role. Change the freeze. I know what to do, what I have to say.

"You should leave," I tell my father.

"Calle, I…" he tries, can't finish, and runs his hand through his mop of hair. It looks unwashed. I study him. Slumpy shoulders.

Rumpled clothes. Inked bruises under his hollowed eyes. My father. Not handsome like his picture. Not the polished-on-his-best-behavior handsome from the pizza place. This handsome has grown tired. A shadow. Used up.

"We should talk," he says, finally.

"I don't think we need to talk. Not now," I say, making sure my eyes don't give me away—it's always the eyes. I open the door wider. "Go."

His eyes flit from me to my mother and back to me, and I see something dark cover them. "Don't do this." His syllables are ragged now, broken.

"Go, Jake," my mother says, and I hear the sameness of our voices. "Or I'll call the police."

His eyes lock with hers a last time, haunted, and I see the loss in them. This isn't drama—this is my life. I'm not playing games. There is no end of scene, no curtain. I just need him to go. I turn away as he pushes past me and out into the night.

I close the door and look at my mother, still feeling the brush of his raincoat on my arm.

"I'm sorry. I've been talking to him."

She comes to me and wraps me in her jasmine smell. "I know, sweetheart. He told me. But it's not your fault. It's nobody's fault. He always finds us."

"He's been here for awhile," I tell her, my face buried in her hair.

"I know. It's why Rob left."

"What?" I look up at her.

She brushes at my tears and holds my shoulders tight. "A few weeks before Rob left, he started getting weird calls at work.

Threatening calls. That's always my cue. To leave. Your father was always jealous. He was like that with all of them."

"All of them?"

"Ted, Dan, all of them. He threatened them. I guess I wasn't worth sticking around for to find out if he was serious or not." Her smile is watery and sad. She continues, "He'd get out of jail, track us down, start bugging the guy I was with. I just made sure we stayed one step ahead."

"But we didn't leave this time." I look around the apartment, noticing the prints on the wall, Alexa's picture. A blender. My mom bought a blender for her smoothies. The only appliance that moves with us is the TV, but she bought a blender.

"I like it here," she says, sighing and combing at her tangled hair with her fingers. "And you liked it here so much. Had all your friends. I thought maybe I could handle it. Handle him."

"But now…" I don't want to finish.

She shakes her head. "It's too hard. He's too unpredictable. With the drugs. He gets violent. I can't take that risk."

She sees my face crumble. I sit on the couch, holding my face in my hands.

My mother sits beside me, her arm warm across my shoulders. "I'm sorry, Cal. Damn it, I wanted this to be different. I really did. But that's why I didn't want to tell you. No kid needs to know she's got such a screwed-up dad. It was easier to just let you think he left us."

"That wasn't easy at all," I say, my words muffled.

"I know. I'm sorry."

"He said you did drugs." I pause, looking at her. "Is that true?" I wipe the tears away, willing my eyes to dry up. She looks at her hands, and I know the answer.

She sighs again. "It was a long time ago. Before you were born. But that's over. It was over as soon as I knew I was having you." She takes both my hands. "I promise. But with your father…it can never be over with him."

I look toward the door, thinking about him out there somewhere. "Should we call the police?"

"I'll call them," she says, standing. "Have them do a drive-by. It will be enough to chase him off for a while, in case he's watching the house. He's not real brave, your father, despite all his threats." She starts toward the phone and then turns to look at me. "We have to pack, Calle. Then we have to leave."

I shake my head, tears resurfacing.

She tries to look sympathetic, but I can see her already moving on, boxes packed. "We have to," she says. "Honey, I know you like it here, but we can't wait for him to do something stupid. We have to leave."

My world is ending again.

"No," I say, not meeting her eyes.

A brief flicker of annoyance moves across her face. "What?"

"I'm not going."

"Of course, you're going." She moves to the kitchen and begins to pull things from shelves.

"No, Mom," I say, louder now, more forceful. "You can go, but I'm staying. You can't keep doing this to me."

She turns from where she has been winding the blender's cord around its base. "You can't stay."

"I'll stay with Alexa. She would totally let me." The plan is already formulating itself. I could actually stay. I could do it.

She sets down the blender and looks hard at me. "No way. I won't let you. Besides, you couldn't afford to stay."

"I'll get a job."

"It costs a lot to live. You don't know." She dismisses me with a wave and walks toward the bedroom.

"I can make eight bucks an hour as well as you can," I say. "It's not hard."

I can see the hurt in her face as she turns to me. "Pack your things, Calle Lynn."

"Everything's about you!" I scream at her. "You never think of me."

"I've spent my life thinking about you. Always about you!" she yells back. "You were the reason this all started in the first place."

I take a step back, as if slapped. "You're blaming me?"

"You're the reason I'm running. He's not coming after me—he's coming after you." Her voice echoes off the walls.

"And you hate that. You hate that he wants me and not you."

"You have no idea what I've given up for you. To protect you. I didn't ask for this life!" Tears race down her face. We have never, never fought like this, and my world whirls with it.

"I'm not going!" I tell her, yanking open the door. "You can leave. You should have left me anyway, when you left him!"

Without waiting for a response, I run through the open door

and into the night. My feet pounding the street, I hear her calling after me. I keep running. I race down streets, no sense of where I'm going, not caring. Soon her voice fades, and I can only hear my heart pounding in my ears.

CHAPTER 25
LAST DANCE

My mother and I pack everything into the brown boxes we found behind the Safeway, listening to Sarah McLachlan's *Surfacing* album, the way we always do, always replaying the last song, no lyrics, just Sarah playing that sad, lonely piano because that's how we always feel at the end...like there are no words...

I CALL CASS FROM THE phone at the Gas and Save. The guy in the Clash T-shirt working behind the counter plays his Game Boy and pretends he's not slipping glances in my direction. When I hand him the phone, he gives me a free pack of gum and goes back to his game.

Minutes later, Cass pulls her truck out front and honks the horn.

I thank the guy for the gum and go outside. Pulling open the truck's heavy door, I crawl inside. "Hi," I say, my voice unsteady, ragged.

"Sam's at the bar," she says, pulling out onto the street.

"Thanks."

She looks sideways at me. "You okay? You sounded weird on the phone. And you look like crap."

"I'm fine," I say, watching the night out the window.

"You don't look fine."

Maroon Five's "She Will Be Loved" begins to play on her radio, and I burst into tears.

"What happened?" she asks after a minute passes. Outside, the dark world slips by, lit windows from town, spatters of trees. We pass the school, quiet and full of shadow. Another place I've lived. Another place I'll say good-bye to.

Cass clicks off the radio. "Come on," she says. "Out with it."

I tell her everything.

• • •

Inside, Lucky's is almost empty: a man at the bar, two in a corner booth with half-drained beers. The country music is low enough to hear the floorboards creak when we walk in. Cass's uncle is behind the bar, talking in low whispers with the bar guy, Harper from Burger Mania. They both wave to us, quick identical salutes.

"He's back there," her uncle says, pointing to a booth where Sam sits, staring down at the empty table.

"Go ahead," Cass says. "I'll get you something to drink." She stops and clutches my sleeve. "And you're soaking wet. I'm getting you a sweatshirt."

I slide into the booth across from him. He starts, clearly unaware that we'd come in. "Hey," he says. "Thanks for coming."

A Band-Aid covers the cut on his head. "You should have that looked at," I say.

He shrugs. "I've been hit worse in football."

Cass sets two sodas in front of us and hands me a black-hooded sweatshirt. "Go easy on her," she says to Sam. "She's had a worse day than you have."

I change in the bathroom.

Back at the table, Cass is sitting next to Sam. He looks at her affectionately. A pang of something catches my stomach off guard.

Cass sees me and stands, ruffles Sam's hair and then disappears behind the swinging door. He watches her leave, his eyes warm.

"Are you in love with Cass?" I ask him, vocalizing my fear. It had been fear shooting through my stomach. Nothing matters now, so I will just ask questions as they come to me.

"What?" He drinks half his drink in one gulp, his eyes genuinely surprised. "What are you talking about?"

I look toward the swinging door, which now hangs motionless. "I don't know, Sam. I don't know anything. I just thought maybe that was part of our issue. Not just Amber, but Cass."

He peels the paper off a straw and stirs his drink. "I'm not in love with Cass," he says, an odd smile playing at his lips.

"Then what?"

He frowns. "Take a walk with me?" A frustrated groan escapes me. I don't have time for this, not tonight. He leans forward. "Come on," he says. "Take a walk with me."

"Fine." I follow him out of the bar.

• • •

He leads me down a rickety set of wooden steps out behind the bar. The rain clouds have thinned, parting like curtains for the fat, glowing moon, which is almost full. Stars peek out in sections of dark sky. Below, the moonlight casts silver patches on the water and reveals a tiny thumbnail-shaped beach, frosted silver in the light.

"Wow," I breathe, the sound of the waves strong in my ears, the taste of salt on my lips.

"I know," Sam says, stopping and gazing at the moonlit world. "Beautiful."

We scramble halfway down the wet stairs to a flat rock the size of a small swimming pool. It has a bit of an overhang, so it's not too wet to sit on.

"Let's sit here, okay?" Sam says, settling in the middle of it.

"Okay." I sit next to him, shivering in the clean, damp air.

"Are you cold?"

"I'm okay," I say.

"So," he starts. "About Cass."

"Yeah?"

Sighing, he looks sideways at me. "I'm trusting you with this, Calle. You're part of this now. People don't know this, okay?" I nod, my heart racing. "Okay," he says, burying his hands in his pockets. "You're probably wondering why Cass and I are so close, right? I mean, we're pretty different."

"You're from different planets."

He laughs. "I used to think that too. I did. But I don't anymore." He pauses. "We're the same, really."

"How?" I ask.

"Cass is my sister. My half-sister."

"What?" His statement sends the events of my evening spinning out of my head. "Are you serious?"

"Let me explain," he says.

I sit back, waiting. He might as well have just told me that he is an alien from Pluto.

He takes a deep breath. "A year ago, when I was in eighth grade, my mom got really bad. She's always had episodes and bad days, but this went on all winter. She has severe depression. We know that much. And there's medicine for it. Drugs. We're still trying to figure out what else is going on with her. She doesn't have typical depressive behavior. My dad finally took her to see someone in San Francisco, when I missed all that school, remember?"

Nodding, I say, "What does this have to do with Cass?"

"I'm getting there." He continues, "That eighth-grade winter, my mom tried to drown herself."

"What?"

His eyes rim with tears. I put my hand on his back, rubbing small circles. "No one knows. It was here at this beach."

I look down at the silvery sand, the dark waves. "What happened?"

His eyes grow distant with memory. "It was night. Maybe eleven or even midnight," he says, gazing down at the waves. "She left the house and came here, tried to drown herself in the water. But someone pulled her out."

"Cass?"

He shakes his head. "Cass's mom. She must have been sitting on the rocks below somewhere. She pulled my mom out of the water and wrapped her in blankets." His eyes are clear now with the telling of the story. "Then she put her in Cass's truck and drove her to our house."

"She could have been caught," I whisper.

Sam nods. "I know. She risked everything. And when she got to our house, my dad just flipped out. Started screaming at her. Told her she knew she wasn't supposed to be there, that he had told her to never come there again."

"Again?" I continue to rub circles on his back, the wool warm now beneath my hand.

"Yeah. It all came out then. Sarah, that's Cass's mom, got really pissed and started screaming back—that she'd loved him, that he'd lied to her. And that's when she told him about Cass. Right there. In our living room. With my mother upstairs in her bed and the ambulance on the way. Cass and I were just sitting there on the couch."

"They had an affair?"

He nods, wiping his eyes. "While my mom was pregnant with me. That night after my mom tried to drown herself, he gave Sarah a bunch of money to leave. To not say anything. So she took the money and left. When he tried to give Cass money, she said to screw himself and said she'd been fine without a father for thirteen years, and she didn't need some coward prick to be her father."

"Sounds like Cass."

He sighs, drained. "Yeah. And the thing is, it's hard enough for me with all of this, but Cass has nobody. My dad acts like she isn't alive, and if I try to talk to him about her or Sarah, he flips out and tells me it would kill my mom if she knew. And he's right. The only one I can talk to is Cass."

"She's a good friend," I say. Another loss. One more person I'll probably never talk to again after tonight.

"She is." He pauses. "I'm not though."

I stare at the water. I can't bring myself to lie to him.

After a moment, he asks, "You know the worst part of living in a small town?" I shrug. He says, "The groups. I've grown up with all the kids at our school, but since fifth grade or so, we all sort of sectioned off. And I've been only friends with this one group. You know, Amber's crowd, the athletes. Like you are with the drama kids."

"This is the first year I've been a drama kid," I say. "In the past, I was always my own crowd."

"But that's the best way," he says. "Because now I'm stuck in that group, and I have to live with their expectations of me. If they knew about all of this with Cass…with her mom and my dad…" he trails off. "I don't know what they'd do. I mean, look what happened with that picture of you."

Sighing, I stop rubbing his back, but before I can tuck my hand away in my pocket, he takes it in his. I look at him closely. "Why are you telling me now?"

"Ever since you came here, ever since that day at the beach, I feel like I can be myself with you. I can really talk to you. I've been wanting to tell you." He stops, looks out over the water. "I just knew I had to tell you about me, about Cass, about my mom. I just didn't know how. Until now."

He leans in and kisses me, and my body warms with him. He smells of salt and a musky shampoo. "Wait," he says, pulling away. "I brought something."

He fishes through his jacket pockets, producing an iPod. He sets it carefully on the rock with tiny speakers next to it. It begins to play Van Morrison's "Sweet Thing," subdued, but loud enough.

"I love this song," he tells me. "I know you love old music, and I wanted to play it for you while I tell you something."

My breath in my throat, I nod. The sweetness of him fills me; he brought props—he thought this out even after the afternoon he had today. He thought of me. Of music for me.

"Look," he says, "I want to be with you. I really do, but I'm…"

"Scared."

"Calle, you don't understand. It's different for you."

"How is it different? I don't care if people see us together. I'm not afraid of what they will think about us. Is that how it's different?"

He looks at his hands. "It's hard to explain."

My temper sparks. "Because I'm not the right girl—the right shape, the right laugh, the right hair. I'm not in the right group. You won't talk to me at school. You pretend you don't know me in front of your friends. You know what? You say they'll judge you, but you care what they think. That makes you a coward, which is worse than what they are."

He doesn't say anything, just looks at me sadly, his eyes lit with the moon. Looking at him, I realize he is not a reason to stay.

"You're right," he says.

"What?" I didn't expect him to agree with me.

"I'm a coward. Like father, like son, right?" He shakes his head. "You don't deserve this."

"What?" I can't believe he's admitting this, but he's right—I don't.

"You don't deserve how I've treated you."

"You're right. I don't."

He runs his hands through his hair. "You know, Cass says the same thing. That I'm a coward. Like my dad. But I don't know if I can be who you want me to be."

I soften and take his hand. "Be the guy at the beach that first day. Be who you were when you wrote me that song."

His eyes widen. "You knew I wrote that? You never said anything."

"Neither did you." Then, I whisper:

"I know that you are drifting, girl,
And look, I'm drifting too.
Only you don't know I'm feeling
Like I can't live without you."

"Wow. You, like, memorized it." There is a flash of something across his face, a quick glimpse of bright moon through cloud cover.

"No one's ever written me a song before." I try to hold his gaze.

"It's not a very good song." He dips his head. "But I thought with how much you like songs…well, I thought someone should write one for you."

"Thank you."

He takes a deep, sudden breath. "Cass says that I use that group like a crutch. That they aren't me. But they're what I know." He shrugs. "I know she's right. I do."

"Cass is a smart girl."

"She's incredible."

"And look what they think of her."

"But they're my friends."

"You don't have to be friends with them," I say. "You're not your dad, Sam. You told me that day on the beach that you wish you could start over. Starting over…" I pause to collect all the thoughts whirling about in my head and try to put them in order. "I have started over so many times, so many different schools. But you don't have to move to a new town to start over. You don't have to play football if you don't want to or go to their parties or eat lunch with them.

"School is so weird because it's like a hundred little universes. I've learned that much from all my different places. I've hung out with kids who do band or they're into anime or they read fantasy all the time or they do sports or aikido or drama or student council. And honestly, most of them don't know or care about what's going on with anyone else. They're too into their own thing. There are people in our school who wouldn't torture you because you don't have a perfect life. None of us have perfect lives."

He sighs and shakes his head. "Sometimes, I think I might just get out of bed, part my hair down the middle, come to school and sit on the other side of the room, eat lunch in the band room or something. Study and get good grades. Never set foot in the weight room. I think I could do that. But I show up and chicken out, you know. I don't know if I can do it."

"Well, I wouldn't part your hair down the middle," I say, smiling, but he doesn't laugh, doesn't smile back. Poor Sam. He seems so lost, sitting here. "You don't have to change who you are, Sam. You just aren't them. You can still play football and lift weights and wear your grandpa's jacket and not be what they think you should be. Just don't date Amber. Don't care what they think. Just be you."

He's quiet for a minute. "I'm not totally sure I know who that is."

"You will," I say. "And I won't tell anyone. About you and Cass. Everyone deserves to have secrets. To have time to figure themselves out. I think we're all just trying to figure ourselves out. I mean, I think that's sort of the point of being a kid. Or a person. My mom's still trying to figure it out."

As I stroke my thumb across the back of his hand, he says, "I just need another chance."

Now it is my turn to look sad. I had lost my evening, my life, in his story, and it all comes crashing back. I'm leaving. Even with my fit tonight, as good as it felt to say those things to my mom, I know I'll be getting in that car and driving away. "I can't, Sam."

He nods, hurt, and pulls his hand away. "I was afraid of that."

I shake my head and take his hand back. "No. Not because I won't give you a chance. But because we aren't staying here."

He looks sharply at me. "What?"

"I wanted to come tonight and see you, to hear what you had to say, but mostly to tell you good-bye. My mom and I are leaving tomorrow morning. And I don't know where we're going."

"Why? I thought the job was working out. The apartment was fine."

"They are fine." I find my own pockets and stare out at the water, Van Morrison low in my ears. "It's not that."

I tell him. Everything. The meeting at the coffeehouse, the miniature golf, the scene I walked into tonight. My father selling drugs, our running from him. I watch his face as I talk, taking in all the shadows, the line of his jaw, the fullness of his lower lip. My stomach clenches like a fist.

Throughout my telling, his face pales, becoming as washed as the moonlight. "Can't the police do something? A restraining order or something?"

"I told her I was staying, that I'd live with Alexa, but that's crazy, right?"

"No." He shakes his head, his eyes lighting with possibility. "No, you could stay. A lot of kids do it, stay with friends to finish high school."

"What kids?" Maybe I could stay?

He looks at his hands. "Well, I don't really know any, but I've seen it on TV."

I look away, swallowing my reality. Ready to face it. "I don't think I can. I'd never see her. She would just be gone. It's too hard. I mean, you understand about that."

He nods, his eyes once again on the night water. "Yeah."

We listen to the waves, deflated.

"So, that's it?" he asks. "You're just gone? Out of my life?"

"I guess." A numbness begins to set over me. It spreads like water filling the cracks of a sidewalk, each limb, each finger, each toe going numb. I have felt this before, and I hope it takes over the whole of me, so I won't have to feel the ache that is fighting for air underneath it.

"It's not fair," he says.

"I know." The ache scratches its way to my surface.

"Will we…can we write, email, call?" He stumbles through each option, aware of how insufficient they feel.

My heart thumps in my chest and crushes my lungs. I can't breathe, but I try to sound strong. "Email, sure. When I can get to a computer, for sure. I'll email you."

He nods and fiddles with his iPod again. Springsteen's "Secret Garden" begins to play. I love this song so much. I can't believe that he's playing this song, that I have to leave this boy behind who plays me Van Morrison and Springsteen and writes me my own song. This boy who maybe loves me, even if he can't figure out how to show it.

He stands, then reaches and pulls me to my feet.

"Come here," he says, holding me closer.

I melt into the soft wool of his jacket and sway to the music all around us—Springsteen, but also the waves and the sounds of the night birds over the water. In this, our only dance together, I am the closest to him I've ever been, but I've never felt more alone.

• • •

At home, my mother sits on the couch in the dark living room. She stands as I shut the door behind me.

"I looked everywhere for you," she says, her voice thin and tired. "I couldn't find you." She has clearly been crying.

"I'm sorry."

"I was so worried," she takes a step forward. "Calle, I…"

"We can go, Mom. I know we need to go."

She pulls me to her, her hand rubbing my hair like she did when I was a child, over and over.

A clock sits atop a box. It's the only thing she hasn't packed. It reads 2:06.

Tick, tick, tick.

. . .

In the yellow light of the street lamp, the night filling again with cloud cover, we pack the gray Honda Civic my mom bought three weeks ago, taking only the essentials, and climb into our seats. Pulling away from the dark apartment, my mom pushes the *Almost Famous* soundtrack into the CD player. I stare straight ahead as we drive away, a sleeping Andreas Bay slipping by us. At the first gas station, we pull over.

"Get me a Snickers and a bottle of water, okay?" My mom hands me a ten.

As we push open the doors, a highway patrolman pulls in to fill up his tank. He smiles at my mom. "Late night?" He nods at me.

"We're heading out," my mom says lightly. "Trying to get an early start."

"South 1 is going to be blocked for a couple of hours," he tells her. "I hope you weren't going that way."

"Why?"

"There was an accident. A Ford Escort hit a tree. It's a mess."

"We're going north," she tells him, but I see her face.

We get back in the car and go south.

. . .

We see the lights first.

A white spotlight and flashing red and blue from the emergency vehicles illuminate the dark trees on the side of the highway, the colors jagged and scattered. My mom pulls off the road when the cop standing in the street motions her aside. Up ahead, a black Ford Escort is crumpled against a tree. We get out of the car. Shards of glass glitter on the ground, catching the light of the police cars, the fire truck. An ambulance is parked near a cluster of men on the ground.

They are working over a body.

I know before I see him that it is my father.

"Excuse me, but you're going to have to stand back." The road cop comes up next to her. He has ginger hair and young, sad eyes.

"I know him," my mother tells him. "That's my ex-husband." She pauses, then adds. "And this is his daughter."

"You both need to wait here." He walks away, his face a mask.

My head is throbbing, the spinning of the emergency lights making me sick. The cold, damp air burns my lungs. Someone comes to talk to my mom, but I can't hear them, their voices murmur and hum in my ears.

I float toward the men working on the ground. Red light all around. Or maybe it's blood. They are not hurried; there is no panic about them. They ease him onto a stretcher as if not wanting to wake him. As if he's sleeping. His face is pale and shot across with cuts and slashes. There is glass in his hair.

"It's a crazy corner," a tall EMT says to the little guy next to him.

"Cop back there says there were no skid marks before the tree," the little one says back. He shakes his head of brown curls.

"Poor bastard."·

They slip a white sheet over his face.

No skid marks.

I sink onto the wet ground, the smell of eucalyptus trees strong in my nose. I feel my mom's arms circle around me, her tears on the side of my face, in my hair. Like glass.

"Come on, sweetie," she says. "We need to go."

"There weren't any skid marks," I tell her. "He didn't try to stop."

"I know, I know." She curls with me, rocking. Shivering, I pull her jasmine smell into me. "We've got to go now," she says. "They're cleaning up. They'll call us later today."

Today. The sky is already lightening, a shiny husk across the night.

"He's gone," I say, my body shivering, not moving.

"I know." The hush of her voice covers me. "I know. We've got to go now."

"Where?" I ask. "Where will we go?"

She pauses, sighs, and releases something. In the wet air, with the smell of the trees and her jasmine, with the flashing lights disappearing away into the dawn, I feel her body drain, ease, and become pliable against me. Settle. I look at her eyes, clear and strong.

"Home."

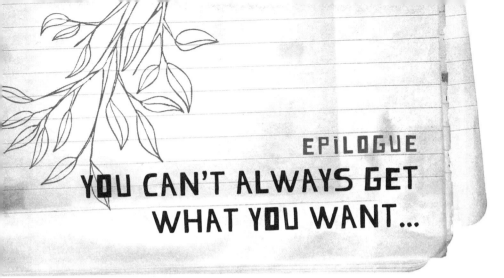

YOU CAN'T ALWAYS GET WHAT YOU WANT...

...my mother does an aerobics video in the living room of the house of a man whose name I can't remember. She sings along with the Rolling Stones song the bouncy blond in the tape has playing in the background and takes an occasional sip of her Diet Coke. Gleaming with sweat, she waves to me where I sit on the couch, reading. I smile at my mother, at her wide, hopeful face. At her sudden energy and eagerness, at her sips of soda between sit-ups...

"I THINK THAT WAS A knock at your door," Sam says, looking up from the copy of *Julius Caesar* we're reading for English.

I finish highlighting a quote I plan to use for our in-class essay tomorrow. "A knock?"

"Yeah, you know. A standard sign of desire to enter."

"Shut up," I say, smiling.

I cross the small apartment and open the door.

On the step is a man I don't know. He wears beat-up jeans, an old army jacket, and a red baseball hat that reads, "Highland Day

Spa," though I'm pretty sure this guy has never been to a spa in his life.

"Yes?" Something in my voice brings Sam to my side. I feel his arm curl around my shoulder, a feeling I've grown used to over the last few months.

"Can we help you?" he asks, his voice lowered.

"Calle Winter?"

I notice the man holds a box in his hands, a battered orange Nike shoebox.

"Calle Smith," I say, my voice catching.

The man frowns. "You Jake Winter's kid?"

I nod. We buried my father almost three months ago to the day. Sam came and held my hand. My mother placed a handful of purple daisies against my father's simple headstone.

"His favorite," she said, wiping her eyes. They seemed small and delicate, just a splash of color against the pale gray of the stone.

"Are you looking for Jake?" I ask. "Because I'm sorry to tell you this, but he's...passed away."

"I know," he says, shifting awkwardly on the step. "He told me if anything happened to him, I was supposed to give this to you." He shoves the box into my hands. "He gave me three hundred bucks. Sorry to take so long, but...I just got out."

"Oh," I take the box. "Okay, thanks."

Without another word, he turns and shuffles away down the street. I watch until he rounds the corner.

"What is it?" Sam asks.

I shrug, feeling the weight of the box in my hands, and set it on our little dining table.

"Open it," he says.

I open the box.

Inside, I find returned letters addressed to me in my father's jagged script. Under these, I find a thick leather book tied with a red string. As if in a dream, I untie the string and open it.

It's a journal.

I leaf through the seemingly endless pages, written with no margins, back and front in the same heavy black pen. I catch snippets of his narrative. "…almost found her in Sacramento. She plays soccer there. I bet she's real good at soccer…" and "…Alyson didn't return my call…" and "…when I get out of here, I'll go to San Diego…to get her, if they're still in San Diego…" Tears drip on the pages, smearing the ink.

"Calle?" Sam whispers. "Can I get you something?"

I shake my head, flipping the pages and reading pieces. Then I come to the end. A half-finished entry written the day I chased after him down the side street at Insomnia's.

I met Calle today. Amazing. She is beautiful and funny. And smart. I can tell she won't let me get away with anything. She's got quite a mouth on her. Good girl. I say, give 'em hell! I like it here. It fits me. I can get an apartment. A job. A real one. Maybe Calle could even live with me part time. I have to talk to Alyson. Maybe we can start things over…

Sam holds me while I bring my sobs under control.

"Shhh," he whispers. "It's okay."

At the end of the journal, there is a CD fastened to the inside cover with bright, blue duct tape. It reads: "For Calle."

Sam takes it from my shaking fingers and tucks it into our stereo.

My father's rich voice fills the room:

"Hey Mr. Tambourine Man, play a song for me…"

I clutch the journal to my chest. I found him.

"…in the jingle jangle morning, I'll come followin' you…"

ACKNOWLEDGMENTS

Thank you to music. To musicians. To songs. We all have a soundtrack in our lives, and each one is tailored to our experiences, our memories, our loves, and our losses. This book is not about the specific songs mentioned but rather the way music impacts a life in an individual way.

There would be no book without my students. A special thank you to all of you. You are in every page of this book.

So many people have nurtured this book along the way—too many to name—but a few specifically are Rachel McFarland, Tanya Egan Gibson, Ann Keeling, Jaime Williams, Kirsten Casey, Krista Witt, Michael Bodie, Loretta Ramos, Scott Young, Richard and Daisy Sagebiel, Caryn Shehi, and Erin Dixon. A huge thank-you to Gail Rudd Entrekin and Charles Entrekin for giving this book its first pair of wings at Hip Pocket Press.

Thank you to my agent, Melissa Sarver, who just gets me, and I love her for it. Thank you to my wonderful editor, Daniel Ehrenhaft, and everyone at Sourcebooks (especially Paul Samuelson, Kay Mitchell, Kristin Zelazko, and Kelly Barrales-Saylor).

Thank you to all the librarians, students, teachers, schools, bookstore owners, bloggers, and other readers who have already been so supportive—I am grateful to all of you.

Thank you to my whole family, but a special nod to my parents, Bill and Linda Culbertson, who handed me my first journal and have been encouraging me ever since.

And, finally, Peter and Anabella—so many of the favorite parts of my own soundtrack involve the two of you.

KEEP YOUR OWN SONG JOURNAL

In the novel, Calle keeps a song journal. She titles each entry with a song title, and in the entry records the memory the song gives her. In the first chapter, she tells Mr. Hyatt that: "Last year, I started writing down memories I get from songs. I hear one, mostly older songs, and I write down the memory it brings. Like glimpses of my life as I remember it. Snapshots."

The pieces of Calle's journal entries that begin each chapter center around her mother, some of them are arguments or places, and some of them are small details that help paint a picture of their relationship. For example, chapter two begins with the following journal entry:

SMALL TOWN
...my mother turns the radio up because she has always been in love with John Cougar Mellencamp, insists on the Cougar part of his name, even if the singer has dropped it. We sprawl on the sloping lawn of the park, my mother letting her lunch break run way long. Light glints off her silver

rimmed sunglasses as she hands me half a tuna sandwich
with extra pickles...

Many people have songs that make them think of a place or
experience in their lives. Perhaps the song reminds them of a trip
they took, or of a sport they played, or of a friend who is important
to them. Music is an important part of our culture, and one that is
also deeply personal.

You can keep your own song journal too! Here's how!

- Select songs that have significance to you somehow.
- Each journal entry should use the song as the title to
  the entry.
- In each entry, describe a scene/memory in your life that
  this song brings to you. Focus on using specific detail and
  sensory description to "show" the memory rather than
  just tell the memory (look closely at what Calle does in
  her journals).
- Create a cover for your journal

These journals make great gifts for family and friends and can be
a fun thing for families to do together. Email me some of your song
journal success stories at kim@kimculbertson.com.

ABOUT THE AUTHOR

Songs for a Teenage Nomad won the 2008 Ben Franklin Award for Best New Voice in Children's/Young Adult Fiction, the silver 2008 IPPY medal for Young Adult fiction, and several other awards. Kim's been a high school teacher for over twelve years and currently teaches creative writing at Forest Charter School. She lives with her husband and daughter in the Northern California foothills, where she often finds her own soundtrack pop up over the speakers of unlikely places like the dentist office, the county fair, and once, the restroom of a Chinese restaurant.

Visit Kim at www.kimculbertson.com